Doorways to the Unseen 10

6 Tales of Terror and Suspense

James Dermond

Ambages Books

This book is a work of fiction. The names, characters, organizations, places, events, and dialogue are either products of the author's imagination or are used in a fictitious manner.

ISBN: 978-1-946038-09-8

Cover art by Jeff Purnawan

*"Come away, O, human child! To the woods and waters
wild, with a fairy hand in hand, for the world's more
full of weeping than you can understand."*
W.B. Yeats, Fairy and Folk Tales of the Irish Peasantry

Contents

The Headmaster

"Rise and shine, Bartholomew."

Bart awoke while lying on his side. His freshly exfoliated face pointed at the wall paneling along the side of his bed as he felt the sting of adjusting his eyesight to a new morning after a night of sleep. Bart remained curled up under the cotton sheets, listening to his grandmother make her way around the room behind him. His nose wrinkled at a scent that he recognized but that was out of place indoors.

Bart felt some fingers touch his back. "Bartholomew, it is time to get up and do your chores. Don't be a lazybones. Your mother and sister need those bales brought down for the livestock." Granny's voice was unusually hoarse, almost as if she had been through a harsh bout of coughing.

Bart rolled over and gazed into his grandmother's face, which was now hovering close to his. Her features appeared blurry, and Bart squinted to focus on what was in front of him. He saw two gaping wounds where Granny's eyes should have been instead, set in her otherwise unmarred countenance.

Granny rasped, "Bartholomew, it's past daybreak, and your help is needed. I'll fix you some breakfast, and then it's off with you to your chores. Don't keep them waiting any longer."

Bart rolled over and bolted up, pushing himself against the wall behind his bed, the palms of his hands flat against its surface. He watched his grandmother motion her head back and forth as if searching for him; Granny seemed oblivious to her injury and just kept talking. "Bartholomew, where did you go? Are you getting yourself ready? I'll be downstairs in the kitchen making some eggs."

Granny stood from where she had knelt at the side of Bart's bedframe and began shuffling past the oaken study desk and stainless-steel coat rack, which were situated by the bedroom window. She was headed toward the bedroom door, her somewhat stooped form keeping its slow pace forward.

When Granny reached the threshold of the open doorway, she paused and looked to her side to speak, "Bartholomew, are you coming or not?" Granny remained motionless, with the profile of her head turned toward him as if waiting for Bart's response.

Bart was able to inspect Granny more closely as she stood in the doorway and saw that her floral apron was covered in bloody stains. Bart had noticed a pungent odor when he first became conscious, but now everything was fully registering following his sudden shock into wakefulness. He could also discern the handle of a butcher knife sticking out of Granny's left apron pocket with a deep red blot formed over the pocket's cloth.

Bart reflexively placed a hand over his mouth to muffle the involuntary scream he almost produced. His mind was racing, and he had trouble forming coherent thoughts. "Has Granny gone crazy? Where are Mom and Sis?" Bart lowered his hand and decided silently, "I have to make it outside. They can't be in the house unless Granny has already gotten to them."

His sneakers were under the base of the bed's headboard. Bart crept around the edge of the bedframe, reached down, and then put them on without tying the laces. He quietly stepped toward Granny and then inched his way to the narrow space between her and the outside hallway of the family home's upstairs floor. Bart could now see from his room that the cream-painted wooden rails leading up the stairs were smeared everywhere with blood.

"Bartholomew?" Granny stepped into the hallway past the bedroom's interior. Her back was now facing the room, and Bart slid past her and the bedroom door. He stopped his progress when he saw that Granny was reaching for the butcher knife in her apron pocket. Granny turned around so that she was facing the bedroom door with the knife drawn and said again, "Bartholomew?"

Bart leapt for the bathroom at the end of the hall, not risking the stairs. The bathroom door was slightly ajar, and Bart threw himself into the small space, surreptitiously locking the door behind him. He pressed himself against the door's white-coated paint, shut his eyes, and took long, deep breaths, before backing away to stand in the bathroom's center next to the sink.

Granny was walking around in the hall at what sounded like the top of the stairway; she didn't seem to be coming toward him. She called out to Bart, "I can't find my glasses, Bartholomew. Help me find my glasses."

Bart glanced down and saw two gouged eyeballs in the bathroom sink and a pair of bloody medical scissors on the counter. The shower curtain was in tatters and had been slashed in several places, while the bathroom floor was littered with tissue paper and other toiletries. Someone had been seized by an apoplectic fit in here and then torn into everything around them. Bart tied his sneaker's checkerboard laces and prepared himself for the climb down from the bathroom window.

He pushed up the lower half of the double hung window frame after undoing the latch at its middle. Bart stuck his head out the window and did a cursory survey of the grounds around his family's farmhouse.

He could see a thick pillar of pitch smoke reaching up into the otherwise clear summer sky from over the hills at Cassville, which was miles away from the family home. As the farmhouse had no immediate neighbors, Bart could observe nothing else and acted to fall from the second-story window.

He lowered himself by his hands from the window's opening until he was flush against the farmhouse's gray siding. Bart dangled briefly from the windowsill and then let go. He fell the short length to the ground and landed in the grass, making a quick recovery to stand on his feet. The smoke over the horizon had now become more prominent with multiple spires twisting in the wind, forming a tenebrous umbrella over the town.

Bart turned the old farmhouse's side corner from his bedroom window to its front and could then view the occupant of the broad porch that buffered the farmhouse's weathered doorway.

There was a figure seated in a rocking chair, rhythmically swaying with the balmy halcyon breeze. Bart's father sat in the chair with his head on his lap. The man's overalls were drenched in blood, and the head lay on its side with its eyes open, staring in Bart's direction but comprehending nothing. Bart summoned the strength to move forward and then kept walking, past the opposite front corner of the farmhouse to the barn, which was out in back.

Bart could hear the familiar sound of an axe hitting a log as his mother and sister entered his field of vision. Piles of timber were near the open double doors of the blue barn, but none of them was being struck. Bart's mother was, instead, removing his sister's left arm below the elbow with a chopping axe; the arm was partially cleaved but remained attached despite Mom's efforts. His teenage sister was standing over a tree stump bent at the waist, holding her arm out, while Mom laid another blow, this time severing the arm completely.

The mangled arm fell off the stump into the gore-splattered dirt surrounding it. Bart's sister staggered a bit, corrected herself to stand upright, and then beamed from ear to ear. Both women giggled obscenely, while Mom handed Sis the axe, before kneeling down at the stump and extending her own left arm over its surface. Their faces were markedly streaked with cruor, in the pattern of dried tears.

Mom glimpsed Bart when she turned her head and abruptly snapped up from her spot at the stump. Both women let out a bizarre keening in unison, their expressions glazed with madness, red-rimmed eyes blazing with an almost religious fanaticism.

Mom grabbed the axe from Sis and dashed at Bart with the weapon raised over her head. Sis followed, waving her amputated limb before her, a thin stream of blood blotting the mowed grass beneath her feet as she ran.

Bart lurched and sprinted in the direction of the highway, which passed the boundary of the farm's crop fields. He didn't dare look behind as he ran—his family members seemed to possess almost preternatural speed. Bart ran faster than he had ever run in his life, even as the thumping tracks behind him faded into the distance.

The highway was empty once Bart reached its paved lanes, and he continued to run. He passed a car that had been abandoned in a ditch, its emergency lights blinking from the tail end that faced the highway from its resting place. Boxes were tied to a rack on the car roof, the supplies of whoever had tried to leave Cassville but had failed.

Bart started to come to a halt only after his lungs began to burn from their exertion. He stumbled and sat himself in the gravel on the side of the highway, regaining his breath after a while, and then sobbing at his loss. Mom and Sis were long gone behind him.

Bart continued to sit at the periphery of the highway, his arms resting over his crossed knees, his brain reeling from all that had transpired. "My God, what is going on? They were mutilating themselves. The same thing must be happening in Cassville." He looked over the pastureland from his vantage point on the road and could see no one else.

As Bart dusted himself off to continue, pressure began building in his right ear, causing him to rub it in hopes of clearing the sensation. The pressure spread to his left ear, and a subdued, sinusoidal humming then became noticeable. The pulsating hum started to overwhelm the ambient noise of the outside and fill Bart's skull with a mounting, nearly unbearable tension.

"Ahhhh..." Bart tried to speak, but no words came forth. The pulsating hum clouded his sight, with the hills, the fields, and the highway being replaced by a brilliant white light.

Bart fell over, hitting the tarred curb, clasping both his ears with his hands. The humming became a dull but all-consuming buzz, so loud as to preclude cerebration. Bart clenched his teeth in agony and continued to shield his ears, in a vain effort to block out the roaring ocean of sound.

Then it stopped. His back was bruised from where he had fallen on the curb, but he was able to sit up in a daze. Bart could feel something moist on his skin, so he touched his cheek. A small amount of blood had flowed from his right eye socket and formed a rivulet across his face, which was now dripping onto his T-shirt.

***

The sun was at its golden hour when Bart passed the "Welcome to Cassville—One Great City" sign after the highway exit. The dimming sun's radiance from behind the stylized, antiquated sign was adequate enough to view the buildings below the off ramp from the highway, which showed evidence of extensive looting and vandalism. Bart could see no movement from either cars or townspeople as he descended the highway's off ramp to the town's main street.

The exit to town was blocked by a pile up of burned-out cars that were smoldering and exuded a gasoline smell, around which were strewn glass shards and the contents of luggage from fleeing passengers. Bart did not want to peer into the car seats as he walked by, for fear of what he might witness.

"Everyone is gone. Not a soul alive in Cassville," Bart whispered to himself. The bright pink exterior walls of the Hen's Roost Diner were blacked by fire, with every one of its windows broken in. As with the highway scene, the cars in the parking lot had been torched, doors welded together by the intensity of the heat.

Bart stood on the steps of the Hen's Roost, which were strewn with debris from whatever carnage had taken place there. The patron booths and the countertop were no longer fully visible, as they had been partially buried in emptied boxes and broken items from the kitchen. Bart stepped inside through the open door and could smell that the diner's grill had recently been used to cook some kind of meat in apparently large quantities.

The double doors to the back kitchen area were open and had been splattered with gore that was now drying but still gave off a strong odor mixed in with the cooked meat and burning diesel smell. Bart pushed his way into the back kitchen and then saw all of them.

Bodies were stacked up in several piles, reaching to the kitchen ceiling. There must have been fifty people in those piles. Limbs had been hacked off, and many of the bodies had been eviscerated. Those corpses that were still whole had been contorted into abnormal, almost impossible shapes, feeding the grotesque nature of the scene.

Bart felt a strong sense of fear upon seeing what had happened and could now guess where the grilled flesh from the diner had been obtained. The floor was sticky and wet with blood draining into the grates between the commercial sinks that had been used as an abattoir. Bart opened the door of the walk-in freezer connected to the kitchen and saw that several more bodies had been hung on hooks, with plastic bags of body parts and internal organs stacked on metal wire shelves along the walls of the freezer.

Bart ran out of the diner and into the deserted street extending through the center of town. He passed more burnt-out cars, ransacked homes, and looted businesses until he reached the parking lot of the small county hospital that was near the next exit to the highway. An ambulance had been overturned and set on fire, and the cars in the parking lot were also burned out. Evening had come upon Cassville, and the only light was from the artificial glow showing from inside the hospital lobby as Bart made his approach.

A number of the florescent tubes used in the ceiling fixtures hadn't been smashed and provided some visibility within the devastated lobby. Bodies of hospital staff and patients had been piled on gurneys and pushed into the open rooms adjoining the lobby area. A faint hissing emanated through the hospital's intercom with the noise of something moving around in the distance being picked up by the system's open mic.

Bart didn't want to risk staying inside the hospital. He thought, "I need to find a vehicle somewhere to drive away and make it to the city. The delivery trucks out in back might still be in one piece. It's worth a shot."

Bart strode out into the dark and onto the lush, well-maintained lawn surrounding the hospital building. A chorus of summertime crickets could be heard, but the environs around the hospital otherwise seemed devoid of life. Several more bodies of patients or staff that had been hurled from the hospital upper levels' many broken windows dotted his path to the loading area in the back of the building.

A body that had been crushed by the force of its impact was dressed in cerulean colored medical scrubs and was lying face down. An ID badge was a few feet from the body's resting place and read, "Douglas Vuković, Resident Practitioner." Bart continued to walk, weaving around the deceased, and then saw the corrugated iron platform of the hospital's loading area.

The loading area's garage door was locked and must have remained so during the chaos at the hospital. An empty truck trailer without a diesel cab was positioned on stilts, blocking the employee parking spaces that were allotted to this area. Bart turned the corner of the truck trailer and saw that one standard-sized delivery truck was parked by itself.

Bart hurried to the driver's side door and saw that it was unlocked. He quickly opened the truck's door and jumped into the driver's seat, closing the door behind him. The truck's cab was unlit, but Bart was able to find a small flashlight in the glove compartment.

Bart had hotwired trucks on the farm, so he hoped that he would be able to do the same with the delivery truck. The glove compartment was still open, so Bart shone the flashlight into its space. A utility knife was in a plastic pouch, and he grabbed it to use as a tool.

The plastic cover on the steering column was wedged tightly in place, but Bart was able to pry it loose with the knife after removing the screws. The bundle of wires fell from the access panel into the barely visible space below the steering wheel.

Bart placed the flashlight handle between his teeth and aimed its light into the panel with the hanging, colored wires. He traced the wires with the color that he concluded indicated ignition and battery, from the experience he had working on older trucks, and found they led straight up into the steering column. Bart stripped the insulation from two of the wires and twisted them together.

The interior lights came on with a jolt, and Bart dropped the flashlight from his mouth into his hand. He found the starter wire and stripped some of the insulation off its end. Bart touched the live end to the battery wires, and the truck engine revved slightly. He put pressure on the gas pedal, and this time the truck revved loudly, settling into a steady rhythm as the engine continued to pump.

There were no lights visible from the truck's cab with minimal illumination from a clouded moon. Bart could see nothing around him, so he turned on the truck's headlights. The headlights flashed on and lit up the concrete divider between the parking space and the line of trees planted in a row near the hospital's outer lawn. Bart heard a keening sound somewhere off in the distance.

The steering column was locked, so Bart searched for the keyhole near the wheel and popped the spring with his knife, breaking the lock. The keening sound was growing louder and was originating from the direction behind the truck.

Bart put the truck into reverse and immediately slammed into something weighty that was not visible from the rearview mirror. He put the truck into drive and spun it around, now facing the loading area of the hospital from where he had found the parking spaces.

There was a crowd of several dozen people running rapidly toward him over the hospital grounds. The keening sound had become saturated and was drowning out the sound of the truck motor as the crowd reached the loading area.

As Bart drove forward to reach the roadway in front of the hospital, a figure sprang from the darkness outside the driver's side window and attempted to pull open the door of the moving vehicle. It was a young woman, whose long hair was partially ripped from its roots, her face streamed with blood; she was snarling and yanking at the door to Bart's compartment. The girl's teeth had been filed into sharp points with an implement.

The girl let out the unnatural, ear-splitting keening that Bart had first heard at the farm and ran alongside the truck as Bart made his escape. She hung onto the driver's side door and took out a large knife with her free hand.

Bart accelerated and attempted to lose her as he barely missed the throng of enraged townspeople wielding axes and bats. Bart heard bodies hit the back of the truck, and the young woman fell off, rolling onto the lawn along the hospital's walkway. The truck was now speeding over the main road through Cassville and then onto the highway leading out of town, its large back compartment shifting and rattling as Bart drove up the exit ramp away from his attackers and into the desolate night.

***

The four-lane highway was flanked by rows of deciduous trees in full summer bloom on either side as Bart drove through the countryside. The night was almost entirely dark with negligible moonlight and a dearth of cars on the road. The chugging of the engine and the wheels turning over asphalt were the only sounds Bart could perceive as the truck's headlights pierced the almost impenetrable blackness before him.

Bart thought about reaching the city, but he considered that it would also be overrun, not knowing how far the insanity had spread. What could have caused this to happen? Has everyone become possessed? "Why haven't I been overtaken by whatever is causing this plague? That buzzing I heard earlier..." Bart hoped to find other survivors, but so far everyone had either become a killer or a victim, besides himself.

Bart flipped on the truck radio and cruised through the AM dials. There was a good deal of static, but Bart was able to find a local news station. The announcer was reading from a statement.

"They are advising everyone to remain in their homes and not to attempt to leave. The Air National Guard will announce when evacuees can be transported to a secure facility. In the meantime, please remain in your homes."

The truck drove slowly up a steep hill and then reached its top. As it made the descent down the hill, the beams of another vehicle's headlights came into view. Bart braced himself and hoped that this was a sign that the city or another nearby town had escaped whatever had infested Cassville and his family's farm.

"No urban center is safe at this time. If you are presently outdoors in an urban center, you are advised to move to another location and seek fortified shelter immediately."

The vehicle's high beams became more intense as they approached Bart's truck, which was moving at a constant pace. The vehicle's occupants were driving at a tremendous rate and passed Bart's truck on the opposite side of the highway almost as if it were standing still. Bart could hear its wheels screech to a halt far behind him and then the sound of the vehicle barreling forward again.

"There are widespread reports of cannibal…" Bart turned the radio knob off and gripped his steering wheel for what appeared would be a fast-moving assault.

Bart could now see from his side-view mirror that the vehicle was a pickup truck. As the pickup truck approached, its high beams shone brightly, making it difficult to see any passengers. Bart tried to accelerate his aging white delivery vehicle with its heavy payload, but he was effectively a slow-moving target on the highway as the truck decelerated and pulled along the driver's side flank.

The reflection of both vehicles' headlights revealed that the truck was festooned with dismembered human limbs and heads strung over its front hood with rope, and graffiti spray painted over the entirety of its outer body. Bart couldn't see the drivers in the truck's cab from his higher position, but the truck's cargo bed held a half dozen crazed occupants armed with axes and baseball bats.

As their truck kept pace with Bart's vehicle, one of the men seated in the cargo bed climbed to the top of the truck's cab roof and supported himself as the two trucks continued down the highway. He stared menacingly at Bart from his perch and put a large hunting knife between his teeth to free his hands. Bart could see that the man's face had been heavily scarred with sharp objects, almost in a ritual fashion, as well as exhibiting the telltale bloodstained tear streaks he had noted on the girl at the hospital and on his family.

The man was posed to leap, when Bart suddenly hit the delivery truck's breaks and receded behind the still-moving pickup truck. The armed man fell into empty space and bounced off the highway's pavement, flopping into a ditch by the roadside.

The pickup truck was not moving as swiftly as it was when it first approached, so the drivers easily swung their vehicle around and came directly at Bart's truck, which was now stationary on the highway. The length of the delivery truck was perpendicular to the four-lane divide, and its back compartment was exposed to the oncoming transport and its crew.

The pickup truck careened into the side of the delivery truck and spun it off the highway from the tremendous force of its impact. Bart was buckled into his seat but his chest slammed into the steering wheel as his truck spun again and again until it hit the tree line off the highway. He was only partially conscious when he heard a deafening explosion and saw the glare of flames in his driver's side mirror.

***

The shattered windshield let in the morning sun, and Bart carefully sat up in the driver's seat. Bart felt his face and chest, examining himself for any obvious signs of trauma. His thick curly black hair held flecks of glass from the accident, which he brushed out with a hand while closing his eyes. The cab's rearview mirror showed no cuts or bruises on him, and he could feel his legs, so Bart unbuckled his seat belt and opened the delivery truck's driver-side door.

The air was acrid with burning gasoline, twisted metal, and blasted corpses. Bart stood beside the delivery truck, facing the highway from last night. The now blackened pickup truck rested in the middle of the highway, still smoldering. The desiccated assailants lay strewn around the finished hull of their means of attack, victims of the broken fuel line that resulted from their collision.

Bart walked around to the other side of the delivery truck and saw that the back compartment had an enormous crater in its center. One of the truck's back wheels was missing, and his means of transportation was otherwise out of commission. Bart lowered his head, rubbing his stiff neck, and contemplated his next action.

"Put your hands in the air where I can see them. Right now!" Bart heard a woman's voice behind him. He gulped and put his hands up over his head, showing that he was weaponless.

"Now turn around, be slow, and let us see your face." Bart did an about face and saw two young women, one holding a single barrel shotgun that was pointed at his head from several yards away.

The unarmed woman spoke up. "He doesn't have the marks. He looks clean."

The woman leveling the shotgun at Bart interjected, "What's your name? Say something!"

"Bartholomew." Bart let his parched mouth hang open. He saw that the women were dressed in blue jeans and T-shirts and did not seem deranged as all the others had been. The fact they had not attacked him instantly was more proof in Bart's mind that they were sane and might help him survive.

"Lisa, search this boy for weapons." Both women were in their twenties, but Lisa was probably the younger one. She walked forward, scrutinized Bart's features, and began searching his shorts pockets. Other than sneakers, Bart was only wearing athletic shorts and a thin T-shirt, so there weren't many places to hide a knife or a gun. The girl ran her hands over his chest and back and then stepped backward, still watching Bart.

"He's got nothing. Looks like you slept in those clothes. Where are you coming from?"

"Outside Cassville. The whole town has been destroyed. Is this everywhere? Can you tell me about the madmen?" Bart kept his hands up and hoped there was a way out.

"It's everywhere. The radio says that all the cities have been overrun. We can't get a TV station anymore. You can put down your arms now."

Bart lowered his arms and put them slack at his sides.

"This is Lisa, as you heard, and I'm Emily. We're sisters, and we're all that's left of our family. We need to get off the road and to the house before someone sees us."

Emily then got behind Bart with her shotgun in both hands and motioned for him to move forward, gesturing with the barrel. Bart followed Lisa, and the three of them stepped off the highway and into a forested area that extended into the hills.

"We heard the explosion last night and thought we should come down here in the morning just in case. You must be the only survivor then."

"Those men in the pickup were insane. They collided with me, and I was pushed off the highway." Bart turned back to look at Emily and motioned with his right hand. "They rammed my truck, but it ended up killing them."

"Yep, they were insane all right. Almost everyone is now. You are the first we've seen who hasn't turned."

They continued along what was now a dirt path running through the woods. A two-story Victorian-style house was up the hill where the trail ended.

"We're up here. We're connected to the highway by a road that only runs past us and then finishes at a dead end. We have to keep the lights off at night so we aren't visible from the highway."

Bart stepped into the thicket and pulled himself up by the young branch of one of the downward-sloping trees. It was a short climb over the hill and into the fenced backyard of the house. Lisa opened the gate and let them into the enclosed yard.

"We lock this up at night too. We've boarded up the windows on both floors from the inside. It's not a fortress, so we might have to barricade ourselves in the basement if things get rough enough."

Bart observed that the yard had a freshly dug mound about ten feet long near its shed. As the two girls and Bart walked onto the house's back porch and opened the door leading inside, Bart could see that chunks of the porch's wooden columns had been blown away with a firearm.

***

Thin rays of sunlight penetrated the gaps between the boards covering the picture window to the living room. Emily sat down on an upholstered sofa and put the shotgun across her denim-swaddled legs. Bart stood and accepted a glass of water from Lisa, which he guzzled down.

"I could use another one...or two. Where is the kitchen?"

Lisa led Bart to the kitchen lined with cardboard boxes along its single wall, and he drank deeply from the faucet. "I don't have to remember my manners if this is the end of the world." Bart tried to smile at Lisa, but she just watched him wipe his mouth.

Emily turned on the handheld radio that was sitting on the end table next to her sofa. The sound was muted, but Bart could hear it from the kitchen.

"The military has begun burning bodies in mass graves. The Center for Disease Control doesn't know why this is happening or where its source might originate. They are taking no chances, as..."

Emily turned the radio volume down as Bart and Lisa sat across from her on another living room sofa. "What happened to your family? Did they all turn?"

"Yes, my mother and sister tried to murder me right after my grand-ma tried to do the same. I ran to Cassville and saw what had become of the people there. A mob almost surrounded me, and I drove away when I got into the fight on the road."

Lisa turned to Bart and leaned in. "Have you heard the buzzing yet?" Lisa's face gave away no emotion but Bart could tell that she was clearly agitated when asking the question.

Bart was startled and looked at both of them, saying, "You've heard it too? I felt like I was splitting in half, and then it just ended."

Lisa got up from her resting place on their sofa and walked over to sit next to Emily. They both stared at Bart and were silent for a few moments.

"We were eating breakfast when the buzzing started. Emily and I were in the kitchen and collapsed from the pain. The buzzing seems to be out of this world—it's no earthly sound at all."

"Like you, the buzzing ended for us, and we could stand again. I went to the back door to find our parents and stood right there." Emily pointed at the braided throw rug in the entranceway. "I looked through the side window, and saw our mom and dad eating our younger brother in that yard. They had cut his head off with a shovel and were tearing at his bare arms with their teeth."

Lisa stood up and turned away so Bart couldn't see her expression. Emily continued. "I ran upstairs and grabbed our dad's pump shotgun out of the bedroom closet where he kept it. They were finishing the legs when I threw open the door and started firing. I was able to bring both of them down without reloading. I hit the porch a few times. All three are buried out back."

"Why do you think we didn't go mad? The buzzing must be what changes everyone. I bled from my right eye after the buzzing, and all the crazies have blood marks all over their faces—their own blood."

"We don't know. The buzzing is like a wave washing over a shore and then receding. Once someone is trapped, and they aren't swallowed up, it passes over them. The radio has mentioned the buzzing, but there are some who haven't heard it yet."

Bart, Lisa, and Emily remained huddled around the tiny radio and listened as the signal faded in and out. Reports came in over the course of the day that indicated the military was losing ground and had to fall back, as so many bases and camps had been compromised. The radio-station announcer at one point mentioned that he had barricaded himself inside the station building.

"The streets outside are filling with throngs of butchers, parading their ghastly trophies. I am not sure how long I can continue this broadcast. An armed guard was planning to arrive to escort us to safety—if anywhere is truly safe—but they never appeared. It is only a matter of time before those below make it up to the fifth floor..."

The evening turned into another moonless night. The battery-powered radio crackled, and Emily hunted through the dial for a viable signal, but some had gone out completely. The sound of a diesel truck driving and then coming to a stop nearby issued from the road outside the sisters' house.

Lisa ran to the front door and looked through the small window in the door frame's apex. Lisa whispered over her shoulder, "It's a trucker with no load on the road outside in front of the house. He's only driving his cab."

The three of them had been sitting in the living room with the lights off, as electricity had stopped working before sunset. Emily had lit some candles that were placed on the floor, away from the windows, but she turned on her flashlight and approached the front door. The diesel truck was parked directly in front of the house with its engine off, but its headlights shone into the woodland blackness surrounding the home's front lawn. The crew cab was silver colored and bore the company name "Ward Trucking" detailed into its driver's side door, which was visible from their hiding spot.

"Lisa, that's Uncle Phil's rig! He is alive, then! We have to go outside and get him in here."

Lisa put her hands over the front doorknob and said, "Wait. How do we know that is Uncle Phil? Some of the crazies might have just gotten his truck and drove it out here. Let's see if he steps out and shows himself first."

Nothing stirred from within the cab while the truck's high beams shone into the ring of sparse trees at the country road's dead end. Lisa and Emily were too far away to determine if someone was even in the cab at all.

"We have to check. I'm bringing the shotgun. Hold the flashlight for me." Lisa took Emily's flashlight as she returned to the living room to fetch the pump-action shotgun. Bart followed Emily to the front door, and they walked outside together to stand on the lawn a few yards away from the cab's sealed and darkened enclosure.

"Phil, is that you? We need to make sure that you're OK." Emily held the shotgun in both hands but pointed its barrel away from the cab. "Phil, open the door if you're all right."

The door to the truck's cab flung open, and a misshapen man thing spilled out, charging at Emily. Part of its once-human face was deformed so that the right eye had become gigantic and bulbous, and its gaping mouth was filled with sharp, horn-shaped teeth.

The creature let out a hideous croak as it battered an aghast Emily with an elongated, suckered tentacle where its right arm should have been instead. Lisa shrieked and watched Emily drop her shotgun on the ground as she was choked to death by the tendril wrapped around her throat. Bart turned toward the house's front porch to flee but was pulled off his feet by a second tentacle emanating from the monstrosity's torso.

On the living room table, the radio's news broadcast signal ebbed and was gradually replaced by a sinusoidal humming from within an inhuman voice uttered a mantra over and over: "The Great Egg has opened...it has awakened. The Great Egg has opened...it has awakened. The Great Egg has opened...it has awakened."

Bobby's Youth Hostel

I t's been months since I've written in this journal. I've been pre-occupied with applying to medical schools, and now I've been accepted to the program of my first choice. I've gone on at length about this university and its merits, so I'll restraint myself here.

I've worked so hard for this and now it's happening. Moving across the country will be challenging, as will school, but I feel that I'm prepared for that challenge. When I first decided to practice medicine as a career, I was only a high school student, young and naïve about the sacrifices this decision would require of me. But I now move forward to my future as an adult, a man ready to take his place as part of the medical community.

I wish my parents were alive to see me now. These last few years have been so hard without Mom—not just emotionally, but without her financial support too, I'm sorry to write. School will be costly, but with loans and some academic grants, I'll pull through. I've yet to settle on a specialty, but it'll be a lucrative one, whatever I eventually choose. I was always very handy—Mom said I should be an engineer—but now I'm going to be a doctor instead.

I broke up with Allison this past weekend. She took the news quite hard, I'm also sorry to write. I just felt our relationship wouldn't work long-distance and that she would eventually hold me back from success in the medical profession. Her hope, most likely, was to marry well, and I wish her the best in the years to come, even if I never see her again.

I never really loved her—this was the root cause of our break-up, more than anything else. I would go through the motions, telling her I loved her only when she said the same. But there was no real feeling there, only some attraction, and even that faded after a while. In hindsight, I'm surprised we lasted as long as we did, considering that only one of us was ever really serious about it.

I may meet someone new in medical school, though my first year will certainly be a hectic one. I'm not sure how I feel about marrying another doctor. Are such couples likely to divorce? I'll have to do a quick search and see what I find (the answer is most probably yes). But the university is a large one, and there are many students there from all over the country, if not the world.

August 24th

Today was the first day of class. I have "Gross Anatomy" tomorrow, which will involve dissecting a human cadaver. I'm not entirely sure what to expect from this class, but I've already heard several worrisome (read: disgusting) stories. In any case, I purchased my copy of *Grant's Dissector* from the bookstore today, and I'm ready for it.

One of the other first-year medical students informed me that while some of the cadavers arrive at the medical school as willing donations, many others are "donors by circumstance," meaning that no one claimed the body and that the state ended up giving the remains to the school. The cadavers are ostensibly screened for infectious diseases beforehand, but I'm not so sure.

That said, I think I've decided to specialize in internal medicine: either oncology or even hematology, which would make me a "blood doctor." Cancer may finally be cured one day, and I'd like to be a part of that—or at least the beneficiary of some cancer research largesse (ha!).

My assigned lab room is across from the school's immunology department, where some of the program's Ph.D. students conduct their dissertation research. I saw a sign outside their office today requesting blood donations and a cohort of subjects for clinical trials. It seems the department is working on an experimental vaccine and needs to evaluate its potential side effects on subjects with certain blood types. I'm interested in the work being done there and would like to meet some of the graduate students. Who knows, something worthwhile may come of it.

August 26th

Anatomy class was yesterday, and I couldn't face eating dinner afterward. Our team's cadaver is in relatively good shape—I'd guess he died in his forties. We won't know the cadaver's documented age or cause of death until the end of the course.

This morning, I stopped by immunology to donate blood with the intention of participating in the experimental vaccine's clinical trials. I'd never given blood before, and I didn't know my blood type (odd, isn't it?).

The study will only select donors from the 'O' and 'A' groups, which constitute most of the general population, and will screen for other variables. There will be another set of clinic trials later for the

'B' group, and potentially the uncommon 'AB' group blood type. The variant of the virus being studied appears to hold a higher chance of infecting some blood types than others, with worse symptoms for those infected from the high-risk blood groups.

The woman administering the blood draw was quite pretty and is a year ahead of me. She said her field will eventually be toxicology. She intends to return to her native country after graduation and work with her father, a physician himself.

I asked her why she was working in immunology, and she revealed her plans to pursue a Ph.D. in the field in addition to an MD. I have to say, I was immediately drawn to her: she's olive-skinned, doe-eyed, and... well, I'll stop there. It's my hope she was flirting with me when she told me her first name, "Aradhya," (spelling?) and then said, "But my friends call me Andi," smiling coyly. I'll know the results of the tests next week.

September 2nd

My blood type is "Vel-negative," one of the rarest known blood types! I always knew I was special, but this is a surprise. Andi seemed pleased as well and said the department might contact me some time for a study of seronegative subjects in unusual blood groupings.

I wanted to ask Andi out on a date before I left, but she was pulled away by the department's PI after giving me my results. Maybe I'll see her around on campus. Hopefully soon.

September 13th

I was walking back from class this afternoon when I saw Andi. She approached an empty bench with some textbooks, a large flock of pigeons abruptly scattering as she took her seat. This was quite strange—the few others seated on benches nearby hadn't perturbed the feeding birds.

She didn't seem to notice me. I walked up to her bench and then announced, "I would use an old pick-up line, but you already know my blood type."

Andi looked up, smiled, and then laughed. Corny, I know, but it worked. We're having dinner this weekend.

September 17th

We ate at a restaurant of her choosing, a hole-in-the-wall place with candles in wine bottles on the tables. Andi said it was "cozy," but I thought it was just dark. The waiter seated us in the back, where it was quiet, which was fine with me.

After finishing our meal, we talked about medical school, her home overseas, her family, and her research interests. She did most of the talking, as I'm not fully comfortable discussing my past. Her family seems quite well-off, if not wealthy, and I don't want her to possibly dismiss me as unsuitable before we've grown closer. She's beautiful, and I could become quite serious about her.

As the sun began to set outside, shadows drew over our table, Andi's face now only partially visible in the flickering candlelight. Her voice grew distant, and I felt myself nodding off, the lids of my eyes becoming heavy. There seemed to be a second voice whispering to me, even as Andi spoke at length, hissing in some secret, unknown language...

It could've only been my overtaxed mind. I sat up and apologized to Andi, saying that I must have almost dozed for a moment. The stress of medical school, even early in the semester. She said she didn't notice anything and thanked me for listening to her for so long, that she didn't have many friends even after more than a year at school. Andi said she would like to see me again, maybe even during the week if she had time. I was thrilled—I felt pulled to her, and I didn't even consider refusing.

December 10th

My final exams are done. My grades have been slipping as I've been spending more time with Andi, but I still feel confident I'll finish in the top quarter of my class this semester. Onto the next set of courses.

Andi and I have been meeting each other as time allows, she being more studious than even myself. We've gone on several more dates around town, and I hope to see her again once we return from winter break. She said she'll be flying home for the next few weeks to visit her parents.

I think about her often when we're not together, which is distracting. I wouldn't say it's an obsession; more of an infatuation. She's shown up in some of the dreams I can hazily recall after waking, and I find myself daydreaming about her even in class (bad). Things will ramp up next semester, but I want to keep seeing her. I can think of almost nothing else.

January 7th

I met Andi yesterday after class and she said she wanted a break for a few months. That we both needed to focus more on school. I reluctantly agreed and said we could at least meet for lunch occasionally, on campus. She said she would call me once she found her footing under her current course load, maybe at the beginning of next month.

That night, I dreamt about Andi again, but I can remember the entire dream this time, in detail. We were somewhere in a jungle (weird), at the entrance to an overgrown and dilapidated palace. Andi stood at the entrance and bid me follow her, but I stayed put. She then began a seductive dance in response, her arms sensually writhing and undulating as she gazed at me. The strange, shrill whispering I had heard on our first date filled my ears, and I felt I had to obey...

My overactive imagination! Andi's right: we need to concentrate on medical school and make it through this semester. But I hope to spend some time with her again soon.

April 9th

I spent the night at Andi's apartment last night. We had met earlier that evening for our first real date since last semester. Over dinner, Andi looked lovely and glowing; she had never been more desirable to me.

She also seemed happy and rested, as if she was more assured of her academic progress. We'd met several times over the past few months for campus lunch dates, where we mostly talked about our classes. The last time, Andi had suggested a date night soon, "as the weather is getting warmer."

After our dinner date, I walked her home and she invited me up. She is an amazing, intoxicating woman, unlike anyone I've ever met. I believe, for the first time in my life, that I might be in love. I'd do anything for her and be glad to do it.

June 7th

As soon as my last exam was written, I received a call from Andi. She told me she had to meet with me, her voice strangely nervous. I asked her why the urgency, and she said she had to tell me in person.

So, I find out that Andi's pregnant. She's known since last month but didn't want to tell me as exams were coming up. I asked her what she wanted to do, and she said, "Get married." I'd not wanted it to happen this way, but I'd already been considering proposing to her, just not so soon. And now I'm going to be a father, even as I have three more years of medical school to complete.

June 8th

Andi called me again today, this time telling me that we have to travel outside the country over the summer break. The plane will leave this Saturday, apparently, the day after both of us get our final grades. Andi assured me we would be back in plenty of time for the fall semester, but that we had to meet her parents. "Otherwise, they just won't understand," she told me before hanging up the phone.

June 10th

I'm writing this from the airport. I did well on my exams, but not as well as I had hoped. I've brought next semester's textbooks with me just in case; I can't stop studying even for a few weeks. Andi didn't tell me about her exams or how she did. She must be too worried about her pregnancy.

We took a taxi here and I noticed as she got in that Andi was already wearing maternity clothes, even though it's only been a few months. She is quite visibly pregnant; maybe it's bloating, but it seems peculiar. We haven't slept together since last month (exams and all), so I can't really tell how much her body has changed.

June 12th

We landed in the early afternoon local time and then took a car to our hotel. Andi had apparently made the arrangements before we left. This city is a huge slum, I must say. While there are some signs of modernity, the trash, the beggars, the air and noise pollution, etc., are overwhelming. I couldn't wait to arrive here as our hotel, at least, is clean and well-appointed. Andi says we'll leave for her family's home in the countryside late tomorrow morning, after we've had some breakfast.

June 15th or June 16th?

I don't know how many days have passed, to be honest, so the recorded dates are only a guess. I was able to recover my journal, as it had been left in our rented car along with some of our luggage. I couldn't carry the suitcases – even so, it wasn't really an option - and instead grabbed a knapsack with my journal inside as I made my escape.

I question my sanity after the events of the last several days. I need to write this all down, as I'm not sure what I believe that I witnessed really happened. We left for Andi's family's home before noon on the 13th and drove for several hours. The driving was hard going as it's monsoon season and the waterlogged dirt roads are treacherous.

When I wrote earlier that I suspected Andi's family was wealthy, I wasn't wrong. Her family's "home" is more of a palace, but one shrouded by the surrounding jungle. The isolation is due to her family's lineage, Andi explained when we arrived. It was only later that I found out exactly what that meant.

We were greeted by servants at the gates, who then parked our car in the circular driveway. Her parents were genial and seemed genuinely happy to see me. We ate an early dinner in the dining room and then settled into a room that could probably be considered the parlor to discuss wedding plans.

Her father, who when not speaking seemed very stern, eventually said that the wedding must take place there, in the family home, and that relatives and friends would attend. I asked him when the wedding would take place, and he said "tonight."

Needless to say, I was taken aback. Andi had never mentioned any plans for a wedding so soon. I also didn't see any other guests anywhere in the house. When I asked about them, Andi only said the wedding guests were "downstairs."

After our conversation, Andi and her father withdrew from the parlor and seemed to disappear. I spoke with Andi's mother for a while, who mostly asked me about medical school and some other personal matters, and then she left as well, saying the servants would fetch me soon.

I roamed the halls near the parlor, noting the unusual décor. The paintings on the walls were not what I had expected; one appeared very old, and showed a snake charmer playing his flute, a cobra rising from its basket at his command. Nothing in the home's art revealed the family's religion, and Andi had never said what faith she practiced, if any.

A servant appeared, an old man, who said he would lead me to the reception. I passed a window as we left the hallway; night had fallen. The man opened a heavy door leading to stairs and I followed them down to a narrow hall that wound beneath the house, ending in yet another door and then another hallway. At the end of the second hall was a burning torch in a wall fixture, dimly illuminating a third and final door. The man took the torch from its holder and opened the door, gesturing for me to enter this dark place.

I walked out onto the plateau of a cavern, one which spread out before me. The servant stood behind me with his torch, making sure I didn't try to leave as he closed the door. Below us were dozens of people, the "wedding guests," all holding lit torches of their own. We made our way down a flight of stone steps to the bottom of the high-vaulted cavern, a dais made of the same harsh stone rising at its center.

Andi's father appeared from among the crowd, his eyes and cheeks daubed with white paint in some ceremonial fashion. There were two circles around his eyes joined together by a curved line that ended at his chin. I then noticed that every member of the gathered throng displayed these same face-painted spectacles.

He held out his hand to me, saying, "Here is the groom. Come to me, my son, take your seat and meet your bride, my daughter." Above me, on the stone dais, was a high-backed chair, a kind of throne. Andi's father led me to the chair and I sat down, not knowing whether they were mad or whether this really was some strange foreign custom.

Andi's father then said I belonged to an ancient bloodline, one apparently associated with many places I had never even heard of (where is Lemuria?). He daubed my face with the same white paint he and the guests wore, making the same two circular marks and connecting line. As he finished his work, I heard the sound of something large moving from the shadows beyond the light of the torches, something slithering on its belly.

An enormous brown snake appeared before the dais, rearing its head and flicking its forked tongue as I gazed up at it. The hooded snake was easily thirty feet long and heavy-bodied, long enough to wrap itself entirely around the dais where I sat.

I don't quite remember what happened next. I perhaps screamed or tried to flee—there's a black spot in my memory. My mind... Where was Andi? I was then held by two men, one on each arm, restraining me as the snake coiled itself at the foot of the throne. It watched me, its reptilian eyes devoid of any feeling, yet somehow intent.

The female snake began to lay its brood of eggs, one after the other, into the soil gathered in a loose pile on the dais. Nearby, at the dais's edge, was a copper vessel of some kind, something which could hold the newly laid eggs if needed.

Once the pregnant snake had laid its clutch, it hovered over me and fanned its hood as if beckoning the others. The mob stepped onto the dais, shouting with joy, dancing wildly as if in celebration. They then began to chant—a strange song in a language I didn't recognize, hypnotic, the monstrous snake swaying to its rhythm as the guests repeated its words again and again.

I was led away by the two men who had restrained me to a wood cage fitted with iron bars. They pushed me inside, one of the men locking its barred door. The crowd filed up the stone steps out of the cavern, a line of torches lighting their exit. My prison was not far from the dais, and I could see the snake coiled around its eggs.

The men who'd imprisoned me hadn't searched me thoroughly. I had my multi-tool pocket-knife, something I always keep with me. The snake looked asleep around its eggs, or at least supine.

I reached through the bars of the cage and worked its old lock with my pocket tool's short blade. The lock clicked, and I cautiously eased open the door. Several torches in holders still threw light about the cavern, and I reached for one of them as I approached the sleeping snake.

I struck the snake with my fiery torch. It recoiled in shock, slithering away from its eggs and then falling off the dais. I leaped down after it, swinging with the torch, the snake trying to strike but being beaten down by the fire as I struck again and again. I took my knife and stabbed into its eye, pulling the blade free and stabbing again, cutting its head and throat until, finally, it was dead. The snake made no sound as it lay on the cavern floor, dark blood oozing from its wounds in the faint torchlight.

The brood of eggs. I scooped up the soil around them with my hands, dumping it into the copper vessel until it was mostly full. I carefully put the multitude of eggs into the container, making sure each of the soft, white ovals was unbroken and secure. Were these my children? Was the snake that I had just killed... was that Andi? My mind...

The door from the cavern was unlocked. I made my way down the halls, vessel in hand, leaving the nighttime house as both its owners and their servants slept or celebrated or plotted, I know not which. Andi had driven us here, so I had no keys to our car. But its doors were open, so I grabbed my knapsack and fled into the jungle.

I'm not sure where I am now. They may be looking for me. I managed to find a palm hut after only a few hours of stumbling through the underbrush, and it's here where I write in this journal. I need to keep the eggs warm. When they hatch, I'll be able to be with them—my children—in their nest. So many of them.

It's raining outside, so hard I can scarcely hear myself think. How long will it take? I don't know. Sometimes I think I hear Andi's voice, calling to me from the darkness outside. Isn't she dead? All I can do now is wait and hope they don't find me. Not before my children hatch.

The Children of Seth

T he summer house that Charlotte Evans came to stay in belonged to her father's family. Charlotte's mother never went there, and her father hadn't returned to his family's home for many years. Both were gone, and Charlotte was now alone, an only child. Her aunt on her father's side had offered the place to Charlotte as a means of experiencing a moment of respite before beginning her graduate studies later in the fall.

"I don't like leaving you here by yourself, especially with no way to drive into town," Charlotte's friend, Amelia, reminded her. "I know we've already talked this over, but I still don't like it." Amelia put one of Charlotte's bags on the floor of the house's antiquated kitchen and looked around the compact space. Though the small room was clean and tidy, the kitchen's sink and other fixtures were something from decades past, their surfaces dull and tarnished with age.

"Isolation is what I crave right now," Charlotte said, sighing as she parted the kitchen curtains, rays of sunlight flooding in. "Sometimes, I couldn't even get out of bed after my breakup with Ben. I just need to be alone—no offense." She sat down at the kitchen table and began to rummage through one of the brown paper grocery bags nearby, placed there by Amelia.

Amelia stood by the open door, the pleasant sounds of the woods in early summer ambient in the background. "Will you have enough food for three months?" Amelia asked, frowning as she opened a kitchen cabinet door. Taking out a blue and white box and reading its side, she commented, "I couldn't drink powdered milk. Yuck. I hope you don't starve."

"I'll be fine," Charlotte reassured her, as if dismissing a petulant child. "I think that's all the bags. Thanks for helping me with shopping in town." Charlotte took two cans from the grocery bag and stood next to Amelia, putting them into the cabinet with the powdered milk. "I've got enough food to last until the end of the summer. If I really need to get to town, I can walk. It'll take hours, but I can do it."

"What if you can't walk?" Amelia retorted hastily. "The phone here isn't even hooked up." Amelia leaned against the kitchen counter as Charlotte continued to stash away canned groceries.

"It's a risk I'm willing to take," Charlotte replied. "I'm young and fit. What could possibly happen to me?" She grasped the door to the kitchen and then put an arm around Amelia, hugging her for a moment. "I'll see you in eight-three days. You have a good summer on the water with Ethan. I'm sorry I won't be able to go boating with you two this time."

Charlotte put a hand above her eyes, shading them from the bright afternoon sunlight to watch Amelia drive away. A dirt and gravel driveway led away from the two-story colonial-style house, a paved road then connecting the house to town. A copse of sweeping ash trees hid the house, which stood alone on its own wooded lot with no close neighbors in either direction.

Wandering in the woods behind the house, Charlotte decided to let the rest of the groceries sit in their bags for a while. Everything perishable had already been put away in the refrigerator; Charlotte would have to do without anything fresh once those supplies were gone unless she felt like taking the long walk to town.

The woods were quiet and tranquil, with chirping birds and the soft rustling of leaves in the wind. She strolled along a narrow deer path that eventually opened up into a clearing. In its center stretched a large pond, broad and stagnant, its opposite side lined by dense woods.

Looking out over the pond from its sandy shore, Charlotte noticed how murky the waters appeared. Little sunlight made it to the surface. *It must be very deep at the center*, Charlotte thought, watching the wind churn over the water, tumbling white clouds drifting overhead. *I'll come back later and take another look.*

The old house seemed to breathe as Charlotte walked up its steps, groaning as she opened the front door. *I'm glad Aunt Alice keeps this place in decent shape,* thought Charlotte. *I'll have to visit the elderly couple she employs when I'm in town again, probably in a few weeks.*

***

The house's attic was cramped, filled with musty furniture, boxes, and a worn steamer trunk, a broken strap dangling from its side. Charlotte had waited until morning to visit the upstairs attic and explore its treasures; she'd been too tired after the long drive with Amelia yesterday.

Opening the trunk, Charlotte began to dig through its contents, putting aside threadbare vintage clothing and leather-bound books. At last, she picked up an old photo album. *I wonder why Aunt Alice doesn't just throw most of this stuff out*, Charlotte asked herself as she turned the dusty pages of the album. *These clothes are just a feast for the moths at this point.*

The photo album held pictures of her extended family from years ago, including people she didn't recognize. Charlotte found photos of her father from when he was a boy and then a young man—he'd grown up in this house before moving away, just like his siblings. The black and white photos were sometimes discolored and there were several empty spaces in the album, as if photos had been taken out.

Putting the book aside, Charlotte took the last of the clothes out of the trunk, something falling out as she did. She reached down to pick up a photo from the floor and examined it. Its picture was of her father standing next to a young, pretty woman. He was smiling. In the background was the house as it would have been many years earlier. Turning the photo over, someone had written "Warren and Matilda" and then marked it with a date.

Looks like Dad had a girlfriend before Mom, Charlotte mused to herself. *I don't remember Mom or Dad ever mentioning a Matilda.* Charlotte tucked the faded, heavily creased photo into the back of the photo album and then tried to put everything back into the trunk in its original order. *I hope Aunt Alice doesn't notice—like she'll even check!*

Rising from the trunk, Charlotte climbed back downstairs to check the mail, closing the attic door above her. *Aunt Alice said I should collect it for her while I'm here.* She opened the front door and walked along the driveway to the sheltering trees and the mailbox hanging from a post near the road. She pried open the mailbox's lid and found nothing inside.

Someone was coming up the road on a bicycle. As the cyclist grew closer, Charlotte could see it was a young woman wearing a summer dress. The young woman waved a hand and then brought her bicycle to a stop near the mailbox, resting her sneakered feet on the pavement.

"Good morning," the woman said gaily, smiling at Charlotte. "It looks like the old place has a guest."

"I'm here for a while," Charlotte replied, returning the woman's smile as best she could. "Housesitting for my aunt, Alice. Nobody lives here anymore, and my aunt wanted the house occupied before it's sold. Are you from town?" Charlotte studied the woman as she waited for an answer. She was naturally beautiful, with flowing, honey-colored hair and striking green eyes. A real knock-out.

"I'm not from town, but I am from around here," the woman answered, still smiling and genial. Charlotte considered this answer somewhat puzzling.

"What's your name?" the woman said.

"Charlotte Evans. Pleased to meet you." Charlotte held out her hand, but the woman only continued to grip her bicycle's handlebars.

"I knew a boy named Evans once. A long time ago," the woman said quietly, her smile fading. She turned away from Charlotte for a moment and looked behind her, as if examining the house.

"And who are you? May I know your name?" Charlotte asked, almost insisting, feeling a sudden discomfort at the break in the conversation.

Without a word, the woman began to pedal off. She didn't turn back or offer an explanation—she just rode silently away. Charlotte watched her glide down the road, her bike bell lightly chiming. Finally, the woman disappeared around a winding curve, gone beyond the leafy trees.

Bewildered, Charlotte returned to the house to make lunch, thinking that she'd pick up again with her summer reading list in the evening. She briefly paused, wondering why a young woman would be riding such an old-fashioned bike.

***

The fireplace crackled, the only source of light in the living room other than the lamp next to Charlotte's armchair. Charlotte turned a page in her hardback book, nodding for a moment beneath the fireplace's soothing warmth. The night outside was cool; it was still early summer.

When the professor had gone, Sergey Ivanovitch turned to his brother. After reading the first sentence of the new chapter, Charlotte yawned, thinking, *I can't finish this chapter tonight. Maybe tomorrow.*

Resting the book on the side table, Charlotte then heard a floorboard creak upstairs, followed by the sound of soft footsteps. A dull thud echoed from the stairs to the floor below, as if someone had just put their weight onto its steps.

Squinting in the low light of the room, Charlotte glanced cautiously toward the living room's open door. More footsteps echoed in the hallway and then a shadow fell over the entrance. Someone was there—standing in the hall, waiting. Charlotte's lamp light dimmed and flickered, the fireplace's flames dwindling behind her.

"Hello? I know you're there," Charlotte said, now standing in front of her chair. She reached for a fireplace poker and held it firmly, ready to confront her intruder.

There was a mournful sigh and a breeze gushed through the room, its odor fetid and decayed, smelling subtly of fenland. The shadow then receded, pulling back into the dark of the hallway until it finally vanished.

Charlotte hurried toward the light switch on the wall and slapped it on. The ceiling lamp bathed the room in bright light. No one was there.

Poker in hand, Charlotte checked the upstairs bedrooms and then searched the ground floor of the house. Turning on the kitchen lights, she scrutinized the nighttime yard from the front porch and then locked the front and side doors. *I was almost asleep*, Charlotte thought, trying to reassure herself, her uneasiness still palpable. *It was just a dream. I'm all alone out here.*

***

Charlotte put the house keys into her jeans pocket and then checked her billfold for the cash she had brought with her. *The walk to town will likely take three or more hours*, Charlotte determined. *It's a sunny day, and I can make an excursion of it. But I should've asked Amelia to put her bike in the car trunk for me. I'm just too independent for my own good, I guess.*

She walked to the back of the house, deciding she might find an old bicycle in the house's root cellar. *I haven't looked here*, Charlotte thought as she pulled open its swinging double doors and stepped inside.

The root cellar was dry and lined with jars resting on wooden shelves. Charlotte carefully descended the short set of stairs to the earthen floor and began to search around. The cellar was dark—she could find no suspended light bulb—but the midday sun streaming from the open door supplied enough light.

Against the far wall leaned a rusted bicycle, a wire basket affixed to its front. Standing over the antique bike, Charlotte thought it seemed oddly familiar. It finally came to her: it looked the same as the bicycle of that strange girl she had seen a few weeks ago. Charlotte touched the corroded bell on the left handlebar, finding that it still rang.

This isn't going to get me to town, Charlotte concluded. *I'll just have to walk.* Closing the cellar door behind her, Charlotte joined the road and made a steady pace on foot to her destination. Aunt Alice had given Charlotte the address of the couple who had been keeping her house since last year, asking that Charlotte check in with them at least once during her visit.

When she finally arrived, Charlotte found that the small town was clustered around a charming main street peppered with shops. It ended with a white and gray church, its roof formed into a steeple. Charlotte found a side street that led to several rows of small houses, their exteriors all alike. The elderly couple lived in a cottage past the houses on the town's outskirts.

The cottage was tiny, barely large enough for two people, but quaint and cozy. Charlotte stood on the front steps and knocked on the door.

A withered old woman answered, short and white-haired. "Hello, young lady. How may I help you?" she asked, her smile kindly but vacant.

"I'm Charlotte Evans, Alice Evans' niece," Charlotte replied. "I've been staying at the house these past weeks. Aunt Alice asked me to check in with you once I got settled in."

"Yes, Charlotte. We've been waiting for you. Please come in," the woman said, stepping away from the open door. "Meet my husband, Charles."

An elderly man, stooped and walking stiffly, stopped at the end of the hall. He waved for a moment and then shuffled away, seemingly preoccupied.

"Charles helps me with the house when he can," the woman said, her tone plaintive. "But somedays he's like this. Neither one of us has much time left. But come in."

Stepping inside, Charlotte saw that the home was well kept and pleasantly decorated, with decades' worth of family heirlooms, treasured keepsakes, and portrait photographs filling the living room. The woman slipped into the nearby kitchen and soon returned with porcelain teacups and a teapot resting on a tray. She set the tray on the low table in front of Charlotte.

As the woman poured Charlotte a cup of hot tea, she said, "I'm Iris, by the way. I've known your aunt for many years—she and your father attended school in Winslow. I worked in the school cafeteria, you see. I've lived in Winslow my whole life."

"Pleased to meet you, Iris," Charlotte said, noticing that Charles was now nowhere to be seen. "I hadn't really seen much of Aunt Alice until a few years ago, when Dad passed away."

"Yes, Alice had told us about that. Such a shame," Iris said, her eyes sad. "What about your mother? She was from Winslow as well, you know."

"Mom's gone as well, sometime before Dad," Charlotte replied, her voice full of regret. "But she was taken by a freak accident, not an illness. I always thought I'd see them grow old together, but it wasn't to be."

Iris poured herself a cup of tea and then took a slip. "Your father rarely came back to Winslow after he married your mother," Iris said, her tone becoming steadier. "He lost his first love here, long before her. I suppose that was his reason."

"Who was that?" Charlotte queried, her interest suddenly piqued. "Mom and Dad never talked much about their early years in this small town. I guess they just wanted to forget about it, after moving away and creating a new life for themselves."

"That's a shame, my dear," Iris answered. "When he was a young man, your father loved a girl named Matilda Graves. They were planning to be wed. But, just before the wedding, she vanished, disappeared without a trace.

"People in town said it was cold feet, but I never believed any of it," Iris confided. "Everything she had ever known was in Winslow, and she loved your father more than anything else. Matilda would often talk of the children they would have someday. She's still listed as a missing person, as I understand it."

Charlotte thought back to the photograph she had seen in the attic trunk: her father with a young woman, the name "Matilda" written on its back. Asking quickly, Charlotte said, "Then how did Dad ever meet my mom if he was to be married to someone else? They must have gotten together soon after."

"They did," Iris replied, her answer sharp. "Audrey swooped in, and soon they were dating again. They married shortly after. Your mother had been Warren's steady girlfriend for a while before his engagement to Matilda."

"Well, I don't know what to say," Charlotte said, finishing her cup of tea. "But, like I told you, Mom and Dad seldom discussed their hometown. They were distant, almost absentee, parents in many ways."

There was a silence. Both women peered into their teacups, neither looking at the other.

"Well," Charlotte finally said, breaking the silence, "thank you for the tea. It was lovely. Will you be stopping by sometime this summer?"

"Yes, certainly, my dear," Iris answered, seemingly happy to change the subject. "I'll bring Charles with me if he's able. We drive up to the house. I'm not a young thing like you, you know."

Iris saw Charlotte to the door and waved as the younger woman walked away. Charlotte found her way to Main Street and then the path home. It was late afternoon, and the sun would be setting by the time she arrived back at the house.

The early summer leaves shaded Charlotte as she ambled along the roadside. Her light canvas sneakers were dusty from her long walk and her arm ached from carrying the bag of groceries. Charlotte was tired, surprised that the slow-paced journey to and from town had taken so much out of her. The sun had become burnt orange. It sank slowly below the trees shielding the road from the horizon.

Far ahead in the opposite lane, a bicycle sped toward her. The rider looked like a woman, but Charlotte couldn't quite make her out. The bicycle's bell chimed once and then again, as if warning pedestrians of its arrival. Charlotte turned to follow the rider as she rolled past, finally able to see the woman's face in the dimming light.

The young woman's features were pallid white, like an alabaster death mask. She stared fixedly ahead, not glancing at Charlotte as she rode past; it was as if she was entirely unaware of her presence. The bicycle hastened away, eventually vanishing into the shadows of the first hours of evening.

Shaken, Charlotte thought, *That looked like the girl I met at the mailbox. But she looked . . . strange. Like she was sick.*

As soon as she got home, Charlotte went to sleep, exhausted by her exertions. Tomorrow, she would try to find out more about Matilda Graves.

***

Charlotte frowned as she studied the picture of her father with the young woman. *It's the same girl,* she thought, *the one I saw at the mailbox on the bike. But it can't be—this picture is decades old.*

Putting the photo away, Charlotte climbed down from the attic to explore the woods behind the house again, hoping to clear her mind. The pond was as she had left it: louring, with scores of lily pads and lines of thin foam floating by its banks.

For the first time, Charlotte noticed a moss-covered rowboat, its oars missing, propped up against a tree not far from the pond. The rowboat seemed as if it hadn't been used for many years, but Charlotte supposed it had probably once taken short trips on the water. The pond was large, after all—almost a small lake.

The wind rustled across the water, causing waves to cascade toward the shore. Charlotte then heard her name on the wind: someone was calling to her. *Charlotte,* the voice whispered, its sound both distant and intimate. Her name again: *Charlotte.* It was a woman's voice, but Charlotte was alone by the water.

Near the pond's unfathomed center, a white shape formed. Slowly, it drifted toward the shore. Charlotte peered ahead, the overcast day offering nothing.

As the shape came closer, it began to rise from the water. First, a head wearing a veil appeared, then a woman's midsection, and finally, wading through the shallows, a woman wearing a full white wedding dress.

The woman moved toward Charlotte steadily, her expression partially concealed by the veil. But, as far as Charlotte could tell, it was unimaginably malevolent.

***

Charlotte opened her eyes, seeing the star-filled sky above her. The evening was very still, with a bright full moon bathing the grass and leaves nearby with a soft glow. The sky was no longer cloudy as it had been before.

Sitting up, Charlotte realized she was somewhere in the woods, the pond no longer in view. *Where? The water . . .*

Her head pounding, she stood and peered around. With a wave of relief, she spied the house, its roof jutting distantly through a tangle of trees. Within minutes, Charlotte had reached the front steps and pushed open the door. She heard voices coming from the kitchen.

Charlotte stood at the kitchen's threshold and stared, horror-struck. Two women were seated at the kitchen table, a tea service between them. One was her mother as a young woman and the other was Matilda Graves. They were engaged in a friendly dialogue.

"I'm so glad you could come over to discuss the wedding," Charlotte's mother said amiably. "Warren couldn't be here as he had to help his parents in town. They'll be back tonight."

"I'm pleased, but I'll have to get going soon," Matilda said, "it's still a fair ride back to town on my bike. Warren had a list of things we need to take care of before the big day—did he leave it with you?"

"Why, yes," Charlotte's mother replied, "it's right here. Finish your tea and we'll discuss it." She placed a few sheets of paper in front of Matilda and then excused herself for a moment. When she came back, Matilda complained of feeling drowsy.

"I'm sorry you're not feeling well, dear," Charlotte's mother said, a smile forming on her curved lips. "Perhaps you need to lie down?"

"That's a good idea," Matilda said, nodding. "Just for a moment. Then I'll be fine."

Charlotte's mother helped Matilda to her feet, embracing her with one arm.

"No hard feelings, then?" Matilda asked, pausing to look Charlotte's mother in the face. "You and Warren didn't work out, but we love each other so much. You want him to be happy, don't you?"

Charlotte's mother was silent as the two stood before the kitchen table and then replied, "Of course. That's why Warren will be with me instead."

Matilda grew dizzy and began to swoon, falling against Charlotte's mother. Charlotte's mother pushed her away, letting Matilda fall to the floor with a crash.

Lying on her side, Matilda weakly attempted to grasp something with which to pull herself up. Charlotte's mother stood over her wordlessly and then walked out of the room. She returned with a large trunk sporting thick leather handles.

"You'll fit if I fold you in," Charlotte's mother told Matilda, her words drenched in venom. "But I'm going to take this out to that pond first. Don't go anywhere—not that you can."

The specters faded, and Charlotte heard the ladder to the attic descend with a loud thud. Almost in a trance, Charlotte left the kitchen and stood before the attic's ladder. Slowly, she reached out and began to haul herself up.

The steamer trunk was closed. Charlotte stood by the hatch, unmoving, tears forming in her eyes. Slowly, the trunk's lid began to yawn open. There was a pause—a terrible silence filled the dark space.

A hand shot from the trunk, the fingers distended and claw-like. Charlotte flinched but didn't move. Foul water began to pour from the trunk, forming pools and rivulets around Charlotte's feet.

Matilda rose jerkily, her wedding veil flat against her mottled skin, her eyes bulging, her face bloated and decomposed. Charlotte remained in her spot, paralyzed with fear. She could only watch as

Matilda stepped from the trunk and, in slow, loping strides, drew closer. Charlotte could feel the ghost's chill breath on her bare neck.

Matilda leaned in and, in a voice like dead leaves, whispered something in Charlotte's ear.

***

The sheriff looked down at Iris, who stood next to the attic's ladder below him. She wore a worried expression that changed to one of shock when the sheriff spoke to her: "She's up here, ma'am. She's been dead for at least a few days, given the state of this corpse. I'm coming back down to call the coroner."

Iris stepped aside as the sheriff climbed down. Curtly, he folded the ladder back up and then closed the attic's hatch. "There's no need for you to be here, Mrs. Martin. There's nothing you can do for Miss Evans now. We'll take your statement in town."

Night fell over the empty house, its doors locked and bolted from the outside. The winds rippled over the pond's surface, its waters darkish and foreboding. From within the attic, the sound of sobbing cut through the dark, agonized and afraid. They were coming from the closed steamer trunk, its last memento collected.

Mementos of the Past

"Y ou said you'd work the graveyard shift. That's why we hired you."

Daryl was filling out a stack of paperwork as his supervisor, Malcolm, spoke to him from behind his desk. Today was Daryl's first day at his new job.

Daryl had just been fired from his previous security job for suspected theft and hadn't had the luxury of being choosy about his next position. But this nearly derelict hospital—on the far side of the bridge, in a part of the city he would never have visited otherwise—had been willing to hire him right away.

An employment agency had connected Daryl with Malcolm earlier in the week. Yesterday, Malcolm asked Daryl over the phone to report to work in the early evening instead of at midnight so he'd have time to fill out the required forms and go over his duties. Malcolm had told Daryl he was never in the hospital building during the late-night shift, but that everyone who worked the shift reported to him.

"It's such a hard-to-fill vacancy. Well, that's everything. Just sign here and then here. You'll get your first paycheck mailed to the address on file in about two weeks." Malcolm tried to smile pleasantly as he watched Daryl complete the final form, but it was late and he wanted to be at home.

"Thank you, sir. I'm glad to be here," Daryl said with a modicum of sincerity. "I'm sure we'll have a good work relationship."

Malcolm rested his folded hands over his conspicuous paunch, not saying anything, but still smiling.

"OK. You can grab some dinner across the street at Melvin's—everybody who works late eats there, including the nurses." Malcolm's smile faded. "But we don't want any trouble with them, you hear me?"

"Yes, sir. I'll keep my hands to myself, sir," Daryl reassured his new boss, putting his pen back into his shirt pocket.

"That's good, that's good. If you work the graveyard shift, you won't see too many of 'em anyway. Besides, most of the pretty ones work during the day. The point is, don't get too friendly with the nurses." Malcolm stood and shook Daryl's hand, walking around his desk to see him out of his office.

"At least an hour before midnight, take the elevator to the thirteenth floor," Malcolm reminded him. "Look for Reggie and take over for him once he shows you the ropes. Otherwise, your shift starts at midnight every night you're scheduled unless I say different. I won't see you again for another few weeks—not until our monthly staff meeting on the last Thursday of the month."

Walking through one of the hospital's revolving glass turnstiles, Daryl exited onto the busy street. It was a warm summer evening, and he watched a hazy orange sun drift over the tops of the tall buildings on the borough's far side.

Daryl missed his hometown upstate, but he was excited to have moved to the city and eagerly anticipated the opportunities he believed it would eventually offer him. Would he gain fame one day as an actor? That was his hope.

Daryl explored the city blocks and then ate his dinner at Melvin's. Leaving the restaurant, he sprinted across the street to the hospital's main building, its floors now lit against the backdrop of the nighttime city. Daryl narrowly dodged the oncoming traffic, coming close to a speeding taxi. Reaching the hospital, he paused at the corner.

The corner was different from its companion at the hospital's front. It too was inlaid with gray bricks, but there was a dedication plaque, likely to a donor or the hospital's founder.

Examining the dedication, Daryl noted the hospital's name and a date late in the last century. There was also a man's name: Nathaniel Wingate. The dedication under Wingate's name read, "For our lives eternal." There was a circle in each of the plaque's four corners and within each were ornate symbols and letters, too small for Daryl to easily decipher.

Daryl walked through the hospital lobby and took an elevator to the thirteenth floor. A bell chimed as the elevator doors opened, allowing him a view of the floor's reception desk. Daryl greeted the nurse on duty as he approached and asked for Reggie, indicating that he was the new midnight shift guard.

"Reggie's finishing his rounds. He should be back soon," the nurse replied affably. "But there're still hours to go in his shift. Aren't you early?" The nurse seemed perplexed that anyone would want to get a head start on the graveyard shift, especially on the cancer and hospice floor. Daryl inhaled the faint smell of death, an odor even the antiseptic couldn't hide.

"Yes, but I didn't want to spend it in the downstairs lobby. Malcolm said I could show up early if I wanted to." Daryl looked around and saw there were still staff wandering the halls. He knew almost all of them would leave before he began his shift.

"Suit yourself. You can wait in the nurse's lounge down the hall until Reggie circles back. I made fresh coffee only an hour ago." The nurse gave a tight smile and turned back to the magazine she had previously been engrossed in.

The walls of the hospital looked worn and tired, as if every place Daryl went desperately needed a fresh coat of paint. The doors to the patient rooms were also shabby, with black adhesive tape placed over the odd inset window. Daryl wondered if anywhere in the hospital had been renovated recently.

He stopped at a wide picture window further down the hallway and peered out over the city. High-rises blocked most of the view of the bay, but Daryl could still see the body of water and a small island in the distance. The thirteenth was the hospital's top floor and, according to Malcolm, it would soon be nearly deserted.

Daryl pushed open the door to the lounge and found two nurses in conversation. Foam coffee cups in hand, the women turned as Daryl entered.

"You the new hire?" the younger nurse asked, emptying her cup and tossing it into a waste bin near the metal sink.

"Yes, ma'am. Today's my first day. On the night shift. I'm going to meet Reggie soon." Daryl tried to be polite, but the women seemed to be in on a joke that he wasn't aware of; the older nurse wore a sly grin as he replied to them.

"Well, good luck with that. Not many can handle the graveyard hour shift up here. Most quit after some months or even a few weeks. Some of the nurses think there's something 'off' about this floor." The younger nurse was smirking now, as if unable to believe that anyone would be foolish enough to take this job.

"You don't say. You mean like the floor is haunted or something?" Daryl didn't believe in the supernatural, but he noticed the nurses seemed serious, even convinced.

"Can't say," the younger nurse replied. "No one except the late-night shift guard ever sees anything. The guards sometimes complain that they see or hear things at night. Since I've been here, a few guards have just up and left without warning. Punch out at the ends of their shifts and don't show up for work the next day. Some don't even bother to call." The nurses exchanged glances and then walked past Daryl, not bothering to make any pleasantries as they exited the room.

Daryl stood alone in the lounge, thinking back to his phone call with Malcolm. Malcolm had asked personal questions—if he was married, and if he had any family in the city. No, Daryl had told him, he was single, and his parents weren't from around here. He had only arrived months ago from upstate. Hearing this, Malcolm had offered him the job.

Returning to the reception desk with a cup of coffee, Daryl found a man wearing a blue security guard uniform chatting to the nurse he had spoken to earlier. The man turned and seemed to recognize Daryl, offering his hand in greeting as Daryl approached.

"Daryl!" the man said, giving him a firm handshake. "I'm Reggie. I work the evening shift on this floor and have for years. Malcolm said that you a country boy from upstate."

Perturbed by the question, Daryl replied, "No, I'm just from upstate, not the countryside."

Slapping Daryl's shoulder, Reggie said, "Well, if it ain't here, it might as well be the country." Reggie gave a hearty laugh, amused by his own joke. "C'mon, I'll show you the lockers downstairs and get you your new uniform."

Reggie and Daryl took the elevator to the basement level and then made their way down a narrow hall to the locker rooms used by the hospital's staff. Daryl could hear the building's furnace working in a room not far from the lockers.

"Oh, that. That's the old furnace room," Reggie said, noticing Daryl's distractedness. "The morgue is down here too. The orderlies bring the bodies to the morgue and medical waste is disposed of in the furnace. I don't like to stay down here for too long. The air ain't right."

Reggie handed Daryl a hospital guard uniform from an empty locker and then told him that the locker was his. He then gave him a set of keys and a heavy flashlight, saying that he might need to enter a locked room during the night or that there could be a sudden power outage.

"The lights on that floor ain't so good. Once you change, we'll go upstairs and I'll give you the tour. While you do that, I need to use the commode." Reggie then disappeared around a corner.

Daryl changed out of his street clothes and folded them, placing his shirt and pants at the bottom of the locker. The guard uniform was snug but fit well enough. *I just need to lose a few pounds*, Daryl thought as he crouched to tie his shoes.

The two men walked back to the elevator and Reggie pushed the button for the top floor. They waited in silence as the elevator descended.

"Reggie? What are those symbols on the building, out in front?" Daryl said, almost unconsciously. "I saw a plaque to the hospital's founder. At least that's what I think it was."

"That? Well, that's the dedication to Nathaniel Wingate. He was an eccentric old railroad tycoon from the turn of the century. He paid for the building, but only if it was built on this here spot, facing the bay. Like I said, he was eccentric." Reggie chuckled as if remembering a joke.

"But what are those symbols carved into the stone? Are they religious symbols?"

"I don't know. Never noticed 'em," Reggie said, shrugging. "But there are some crazy rumors I've heard over the years about old Wingate. One is that he was buried under the hospital basement at his own request."

The door to the elevator opened, taking Daryl and Reggie upstairs again. Reggie showed Daryl the wings on the thirteenth floor, pointing out which ones held critical or terminal patients.

"And this here's the cancer ward. You might hear 'em cry out at night—they have mood swings, they vomit. I almost feel sorry for 'em," Reggie said, sighing. "But I ain't worked the late-night shift in years, ever since I got promoted."

The reception desk was vacant by the time Reggie and Daryl returned. "Well, that's it, my man. You're on your own. A nurse comes up here from the twelfth floor to check on patients, but the guard is the only staff member on duty most of the time. We've had budget cuts every year for the past few years, so you're it."

As the elevator door closed on Reggie, Daryl turned about, surveying the three hallways connected to the reception area on the now quiet floor. The ceiling lights flickered. Daryl decided to take a short break in the lounge room.

The coffee in the pot was starting to look stale, but Daryl didn't want to make more. He poured a cup for himself, smacking his lips at the bland taste after taking a sip. A battered TV set was sitting on one of the tables, so Daryl walked over to turn it on.

The television set crackled, projecting a black and white static image. Daryl turned its knobs and adjusted the antenna, but no picture or sound would come in. *Must be bad reception on this floor. Maybe it's because we're so high up*, Daryl considered.

A long groan echoed from outside the lounge as Daryl took another sip of coffee. He cautiously stood up from his chair, emptied his coffee cup, and opened the lounge door to see where the groaning was coming from.

The sound had grown louder, emanating from one of the rooms in the cancer ward. "My God, oh God, save me," an old man pleaded, moaning pitifully between cries. "Please, make it stop, my God."

Daryl stood in the hallway and listened. *He'll wake up the other patients, but they're probably used to it by now. I don't know what else I can do. Maybe he'll stop soon.*

The ceiling lights flickered as Daryl turned a corner. At the other end of the otherwise empty hallway was a diminutive old woman wearing a hospital gown. Her hair was matted and she was barefoot, as if she had just gotten out of bed.

Daryl was about to call out to the woman when the lights flickered again, placing the hallway into darkness for a moment. When the light returned, the woman was halfway down the hall. Daryl could now see that the old woman's face was white, her eyes dull and staring. Her mouth hung open in a sloppy gape.

Horrified, Daryl turned and sped around the corner. The ceiling lights flickered once more, throwing the hallway before him into pitch black. When the lights burst suddenly back to life, the old woman stood directly in front of Daryl's, her face inches from his. She opened her cancerous mouth wide as if to scream, letting out a hideous, raspy gasp instead.

Stumbling, Daryl fell back toward the wall behind him, waving his arms in terror. The old woman stepped forward just as the lights flickered. All at once, she was gone.

Daryl leaned against the wall, breathing hard, looking around in a panic. *What the hell was that?* he asked himself once he could form a coherent thought. *Am I seeing things already?*

Checking both hallways, Daryl steadied himself and made his way back to reception. The elevator chimed and opened just as he arrived, a nurse wearing a white uniform and cap stepping out.

"Good evening, I'm Nurse Gabrielle," the young woman said, her words soft and smoothly accented. "I'm here to check on the ward patients." She looked Daryl up and down as he stood by the reception counter, a clipboard held at her side. "You're new on this floor, aren't you?" she queried. "Are you all right?"

"Um, why, yes, I'm fine. Just adjusting to the late-night shift. Too much coffee makes me jittery. Please, make your rounds and do whatever else you need to do. And my name's Daryl." Daryl then offered her a weak smile, doing his best to stop shaking.

"Pleased to meet you, Mister Daryl. And thank you, I appreciate that. I'll come back around once I'm done. See you in thirty." The young nurse sashayed away, flashing Daryl a quick smile as she turned the corner and disappeared.

Daryl listened to her footsteps echoing past the lounge room and fading as she reached the cancer and hospice wards. He decided to make a fresh pot of coffee and offer a cup to Miss Gabrielle.

Searching the lounge cabinets, Daryl found a jar of coffee, noting the smiling man with a freshly brewed cup on the label. The coffee maker percolated, and Daryl reached for a clean mug at the back of the cabinet.

Pouring hot coffee into a disposable cup, Daryl turned from the counter as the ceiling lights flickered. Corpses filled the room: some slumped into wheelchairs, others covered by translucent plastic sheets.

Their mouths and eyes creaked open, an awful dead-gray pallor spreading over their expired flesh.

The coffee cup fell from Daryl's hand as the room went dark. The lounge was empty when the lights returned a moment later. The sound of approaching footsteps broke Daryl from his terrified, semi-catatonic state.

"You spilled your coffee, Mister Daryl. Mister Daryl?" Nurse Gabrielle stood in the doorway to the lounge, waiting for Daryl to notice her.

Daryl stared in a daze at the muddy pool of coffee on the floor and then turned. "I . . . I'm just feeling light-headed. I'm not used to being up this late at night." Daryl could only imagine that what he had just seen was a waking nightmare.

"I hope you feel better, Mister Daryl. There is such a thing as too much coffee. If it's all right with you, I'll leave you to your duties." Nurse Gabrielle closed the lounge door, the echo of her footsteps following her.

The elevator chimed as Daryl walked down the hallway, trying to shake the vision of the gray bodies. *There's a chance she'll tell Malcolm about this. I have to get my head together.*

Daryl stood at the reception counter, alone once more. He moved back and forth, scanning the hallways, telling himself he just needed to get used to being alone this late at night. He was seeing things, but that didn't mean any of it was real.

The elevator chimed again and Daryl turned. *She's back so soon? Maybe she forgot her clipboard*, Daryl thought, mildly pleased at the prospect of seeing Nurse Gabrielle again. A feeling of relief came over him for a moment.

The doors parted, revealing an empty wheelchair. Daryl felt the hairs on the back of his neck bristle as a profound terror seized him.

Impulsively, without a thought, Daryl walked to the elevator and stepped inside.

The doors closed, and the elevator descended to the hospital's basement. When the doors opened, Daryl stared into a dark hallway, the distant sound of the hospital's overworked furnace heaving and bellowing somewhere in the dark.

The elevator doors closed behind Daryl and the elevator began its quiet ascent. From the shadows of the dimly lit hallway, tortured figures began to emerge.

Many were nude while others were garbed in hospital gowns. For some, the means of their deaths were clear; for others, it wasn't certain. As Daryl stood motionless, the mob of corpses rushed forward without warning. Cold fingers closed around his arms and Daryl cried out as he was hoisted above their heads like a prized trophy.

Half-crazed, Daryl's voice died. As if in a dream, he watched the ceiling blur past as he was carried to the waiting furnace room. One of the corpses near the front of the throng began to speak in a deranged and inhuman voice, reciting a ritual prayer:

> "*We consecrate this sacrifice to our Most Beloved, our Benefactor. The One who will grant us Eternal Life, so that we may again walk among the Living. Accept this oblation, which will be burned as an offering to you, Most Unholy One, Most Unholy One!*"

Daryl was hurled into the open furnace by the hands of the multitude. As the fire consumed him, he could only shriek in agony.

The undead stood before the furnace as it spat licks of fire, the ashes of Daryl's charred flesh floating through the air before it. The corpse who had recited the litany closed the furnace door and the horde of apparitions shuffled away, melding into the basement's mournful shadows.

***

Malcolm stood at the punch clock outside his office in the early morning and punched Daryl out at the end of his shift. The hospital was still sparsely staffed at this time, and no security guard had punched in yet for the day shift.

Turning the handle of the restroom sink faucet, Malcolm let cold water run into his open palms and then splashed it onto his face. He looked into the mirror, wondering whether he would be able to fill Daryl's position without another long vacancy. As he dried his face with a paper towel, a talisman fell from beneath Malcolm's shirt. Its jade surface was covered with strange letters and symbols.

He Sleeps in Death

T homas let the chalky soil run out between his fingers and onto the barren ground at his sandaled feet. He looked out over the fields of pitted crops as they met the rolling hills outside his village and worried that this season's harvest might fail to feed his people.

The specter of famine loomed over Hometown for the first time in living memory. The previously rich soil of the farmlands surrounding the village elder's peaceful settlement was now dry and friable, unsuitable for planting and harvesting. With this harvest season at an end, the villagers came to fear starvation as their once-abundant crops were thin and mealy when finally collected and stored until the next harvest.

Thomas walked back from the fields to the meeting tent, its exterior modestly adorned, with an animal-hide flap hanging over the tent's entrance. He parted the leather curtain to step inside. The remaining village elders were assembled, seated on raised planks around the tent's stone-lined fire, the smoke drifting up through the structure's opening at its top into the early evening sky.

The chief elder had called a council and invited the village shaman as well, lest the harvest gods be insulted. The holy man also claimed that he possessed some insight into why the crops had failed when they had so recently seemed ripe for a successful harvest.

"The land itself has been cursed. Our soil has been poisoned by an outsider." Elijah, the village shaman, gestured over the tent's open fire with both hands, his weathered face lit from beneath by the light of the burning branches. "We have brought this tragedy upon ourselves. Impiety among the youth, lack of observance, there are so many ways to attract the wrath of the gods."

The elders observed his mildly theatrical performance and then Thomas spoke to the shaman, as if interrogating him, "If you believe that someone caused the soil to go sour, how can we find him? Where is this magician that can taint our land so quickly and without warning?"

Elijah became still, leaning on his ornate wooden staff, his voice low as he answered Thomas, "I saw him— or perhaps it—at the edge of the forest past the farmers' plots more than two moons ago. Before our crops began to wither.

"I wasn't sure if it was a man or a spirit, but it was a dark shadow against the full moon, covered from head to foot. The cloaked one stood on the hill and looked over the crops, not moving save for the nighttime winds rustling its long garment. I watched from a distance before he vanished in the blink of an eye; only a spirit of the forest could do something like that. Sinister magic is working against our people."

A village elder seated next to Elijah stood and looked over the men present, "My son, Lucas, saw the same spirit, not long after Elijah. As Elijah said, the shrouded spirit-man perched on the closest hill near the crops and watched in darkness, only to suddenly disappear after a short while. That the crops began to die not long after the spirit's visits can't be just ill fortune."

Elijah prodded the fire with his staff, his bare arms wizened and desiccated. "Some searchers could go into the forest, find the spirit and dispel it, removing the curse on the soil. Hometown may not survive past the next harvest season if we don't act boldly and soon." Elijah seemed very withdrawn as he spoke, as if he could sense the foreboding descending over the council of elders and what might become of him if his plea was rejected.

Thomas gazed over the crackling fire at Elijah and replied, "The Old Ways forbid us from journeying more than three leagues into the depths of the forest. Even a shaman can't change the laws passed down to us by the Ancestors. We might just have to make a sacrifice of forest beasts to the harvest gods instead, profane youth notwithstanding."

Thomas wasn't sure if Elijah had picked up on his veiled jibe or not. Elijah returned Thomas's gaze coolly. "The Ancestors also passed down obligations to thrive and to grow Hometown, to keep this place a haven for our people. If the source of the corruption dwells in the forest, then searchers must go into the forest to find it. Preserving the Old Ways mean nothing if we are all dead."

The elders murmured among themselves, and then the chief elder, Jacob, stood and spoke, "It is settled. Thomas, choose four searchers from among our best men. The searchers must travel past the three leagues threshold and explore the forest beyond the boundary set by the Ancestors. This spiteful spirit may be there and can be thwarted if found. We may starve after the next harvest if the searchers fail to find what is causing the land to die beneath our very feet."

Jacob was said to be a direct descendent of the Ancestors, a man of considerable height and prodigious strength despite his advanced age. His father and his father before him had led Hometown and its inhabitants through many trials, but nothing as dire as what had come upon them with the failure of this harvest. Jacob now began to feel a gnawing dread that he would be the last of his line if the searchers were not successful in their quest.

Jerod entered his family's tent, placing a clutch of game birds strung together by their feet onto its earthen floor. Jerod's wife, Sara, was swaddling their infant son, setting him down for the night in his crib as Jerod greeted her with the eventide greeting.

"Not as many as I had hoped." Jerod hung his bow and quiver near the tent's entrance. "Gage only fell two this hunt. Lara may not even let him back inside their tent tonight." Jerod attempted to make light of their situation, but even he was beginning to worry about the dearth of animal life in the woods near the village. Birds and other small game had started to grow scarce not long after the farmers noticed the failure of this season's crops.

"Samuel's asleep now. Come lie with me." Sara lay on her side across their bed of animal skins, inviting Jerod to join her by running a hand over the soft covers nearest to her. Jerod removed his hunter's jerkin and lay facing his wife, caressing her hair as she continued speaking.

Sara put on a wry expression, the corners of her eyes crinkling slightly. "Do they know why the hunts are failing? What have the elders said? Elijah may have to make an offering to the gods or there will soon be no game left." The women of Hometown had gathered earlier that day outside the fields as they worked, discussing the lack of recent success in the hunts.

Jerod turned onto his back and looked up into the opening in the tent's ceiling, the stars overhead drifting through the evening sky. "No, none of the elders seem to know, or at least they haven't told any searchers or hunters. The village council had a meeting today while we were returning from the forest, so they might tell us something tomorrow. I can never tell with them."

There was the sound of someone moving outside the tent. Jerod sat up, reaching for his jerkin and boots. He dressed quickly, then crept toward the veil of skins sheltering the tent's interior. "Jerod, I need to speak with you. Step outside." Thomas spoke quietly, but the urgency in his voice was unmistakable.

Jerod turned to look at his wife, who was now standing on their bed, then parted the skin flaps to venture into the cool air of the village evening from the warmth of his tent. Thomas stood close to the tent, watching Jerod as he turned to face him. "Walk with me. The council of elders has made a decision."

Jerod briefly glanced at the tent's entrance, then followed Thomas away from his dwelling, down the path between the tents of the people to the now-deserted meeting place of the elders. The two men stood alone, and Thomas reached out to touch Jerod's shoulder in confidence.

"Jacob has tasked me with choosing four men from among the people to go past the lands set by the Ancestors. Elijah and the elders believe that we are being cursed by a malevolent spirit, and this is why the crops fail. The spirit must make its home in the far forest and can be banished there."

Jerod searched Thomas's weary eyes, unsure of how to answer him. "How can anyone change what was given to us with the Old Ways? There could be nothing but death waiting for us in the forest. The Ancestors laid down those laws to keep the people from unnecessary harm."

Thomas replied matter-of-factly, "The council has decided. The Ancestors are not here to complain. I will tell Gage that he will accompany you as well, along with two others." Jerod felt a shiver pass over him as the traditions he was raised with from birth were being toppled around him. To hear one of the elders dismiss generations of his people's customs with a wave of his hand sorely troubled the typically stoic Jerod.

"How will we fight the forest spirit if we are able to find it? Gage and I are hunters, not shamans. We have no magic."

Thomas again seemed unconcerned as he answered Jerod. "Elijah will ward all of you against evil spirits. The spirit of the forest takes the shape of a man, so he can be harmed by those with the ward. So says Elijah."

Thomas walked back to his family tent after reassuring Jerod, asking him to sleep well before leaving in the morning. However, Thomas's outer indifference masked his own trepidation. He thought back to his father and the stories he'd told Thomas.

The people had lived their entire lives within the valley, as did everyone before them. The sun, the moon, the sky, the valley, and the forest behind the valley were the entire world. The gods lived in the sky, and in the sun and the moon. The edge of the forest was where the world ended for the people, and what lay beyond was the rest of the world.

In the time of the Ancestors, there was terrible pain and hardship, but the Ancestors created Hometown for the people to keep them safe. The people would never have to suffer if Hometown remained their refuge, with the Old Ways directing how the people should live. The Ancestors gave stern warning about the deep forest past Hometown and made this as their First Law. Thomas had never doubted the First Law before, but now wondered from what the Ancestors were trying to protect the people.

***

Elijah dabbed the ochre paint in several stripes over Jerod's chiseled face, the mixture rapidly drying in the smoky, heated air of the meeting tent. The village elders and the shaman had assembled again, but this time with the family members of the four searchers chosen to venture into the deep forest. Jerod's father and mother stood solemnly as Elijah finished applying the spirit wards from a ceremonial bowl to the other three searchers' faces, hopeful that their only son's sacred quest would save Hometown but also fearful they may never see him again.

The men armed themselves with fire-hardened wooden spears, sinew-strung bows, and flint-tipped arrows, clad only in the roughest of leathers. The band of searchers planned to set out on foot to explore the uncharted wilderness in the hopes of identifying the evil, or at least finding a new source of food for the village if all else failed. Jerod was chosen to lead the other young men, having honed his tracking skills over several summers of hunts in the sparser forestlands on the outskirts of Hometown.

The shaman chanted over the band as they stood before him. "The gods' blessings be upon you. Go forth and find that which threatens our people. Go forth and find that which will heal our soil and return us to abundance. Let it be so." Elijah waved a smoldering clay censer before the searchers, stuffed with flowering plants that had been grown in his own tent, the plants' aroma wrapping the men in a mist as a shield of protection.

Jerod thought that he had never placed much credence in the gods before today, but now was not a time to doubt their divinity. If Jerod returned alive from this anointed quest, that would be enough proof of their existence to him.

The searchers left Hometown under the bright morning sun, following the single path that wound through the villagers' dwellings, the grain storehouse built from wooden poles and clay, and the meeting place of the elders, then past the fields to the mostly unknown forest.

The dense forest with its towering trees and thick overgrowth in the distance had never held much mystery for the people of Hometown as none had ever thought of traversing the compact parameter set for hunting and for the gathering of wild plants. The Old Ways and its strictures had forbidden anyone from the journey now being undertaken, and no one had ever dared to do otherwise.

Several hours of vigorous walking were enough to leave behind the familiar woods and breach the limits imposed by the Ancestors. The trees here in the deep forest were taller and more knotted than those within the reaches of Hometown, revealing a storied natural history in lands where no one had set foot before. The band of men were soon immersed in the primeval forest, awed by its savage beauty and inscrutable nature.

The searchers took a short rest by a running stream, Jerod drinking carefully from its waters. Jerod studied his men as they reclined by the riparian banks, taking a meal of barley bread.

His mind wandered to his wife and infant son, recalling Samuel's birth just six moons ago. The midwife had delivered the baby, judging him to be sound and healthy. Thomas had once remarked that in the time of the Ancestors, newborn babies were judged as many were found sick and the shamans then had to "return them to the gods."

The band resumed its march up a sharp incline, finally reaching a vista in the forest's plateau. Arthur stopped behind Jerod and gestured to him, with Gage and Sean pausing to see what Arthur wanted. Arthur had a curious character and seemed too glib for a searcher, at least in Jerod's mind. Arthur might have been better suited as a shaman.

Arthur said, "Jerod, that colorful bird sitting on the branch ahead of us, do you see it?"

Jerod removed his leather pack and placed it on the forest floor. "Where? I don't see anything."

Arthur replied, "Look directly ahead and then up, you'll see it."

Jerod rubbed the back of his neck and peered ahead into the quiet mass of trees surrounding them. There, on a high branch, was a kind of bird he had never encountered before. Unlike the drab feathers worn by the fowl hunted for the village roasts, this bird sported bright red-and-yellow plumage, its wings spreading generously as it lifted itself from its perch and glided deeper into the leafy foliage of the forest.

Jerod was surprised, but not overly concerned. "I'm sure we'll run into some odd things as we make progress. No one's ever been here; it's untouched by the people. A bird is probably the least we have to worry ourselves about."

Jerod put his arms through his pack's straps after lifting it from the ground and continued walking ahead of the others. Arthur shrugged, resuming his pace behind Jerod, but turning around to possibly spy the strange bird that seemed so out-of- place in the green-and-brown hues of the forest's landscape.

The unwearied searchers reached what Jerod believed to be the heart of the forest as the sun began to wane, its slow voyage across the horizon spilling light over the tops of the trees and onto the forest floor. Still, however, the ground beneath this part of the forest was almost entirely obscured by the colossal trees' thick canopy, shafts of sunlight only piercing through sporadically.

Jerod and his band came for a short rest in a clearing amidst the ancient trees. Here in the woodland twilight, an astonishing flower bloomed, blood-red in color and sickeningly sweet in scent.

Jerod stood over the band's disturbing discovery, noting that this bizarre flower might have been cultivated by hand as no other plants grew near it on the forest floor. The soil around the peculiar flower also appeared to be withered, as if the flower was somehow leeching more than just its natural sustenance.

"Now this is something we should worry about," Arthur noted as he turned to look at Jerod. "This flower looks dangerous, possibly deadly. Do you think it was planted here by the spirit of the forest?"

Jerod looked back at Gage and Sean, who were keeping their distance as they sat on a patch of grass near the trees lining the clearing. "I can't say," Jerod replied. "We shouldn't try to pick it, even though Elijah would probably treasure it. Just leave the flower alone and we will keep moving until sundown. This isn't a good place to make camp, not even considering that flower."

The band continued its trek through the tangled forest until the dimming sun made it impossible to go further. Jerod decided to make camp against what appeared to be the sheer side of a cliff, the view of the rocks above concealed by the trees.

Sturdy ivy vines grew everywhere on the stone wall, hanging down around the band as they built a fire from broken tree branches and settled in for the night. Jerod placed Gage on nighttime watch, the other searchers falling asleep in the soft glow of the campfire.

Gage grumbled as he felt the need for sleep, resenting that Sean was able to rest first before taking the second guard shift. The band had seen no large animals in the forest, and predators bigger than a feral pig did not exist in their experience, but Jerod wished to take no risks. What might be found in the untamed forest at night could surprise them in unpleasant ways.

Some time in silence passed, and then Gage heard a humming sound in the distance, steadily growing louder. Could it be that funny bird the band saw before? No, this sounded like something much larger than a bird, and it was getting closer. Gage squatted next to Jerod's slumbering form and prodded him awake.

"Jerod, wake up, quick. Something is coming." Jerod rolled over on his woven fiber mat and squinted at Gage. "This had better be serious," Jerod muttered sleepily.

Arthur and Sean hid in the high bushes with Jerod and Gage, not far from the campsite, its small fire now buried under a mound of dirt. The moonlight provided some visibility, but only a faint outline of the forest flora in front of the band could be perceived without the light of the campfire.

As the men stared out into the dark forest, a silvery sphere the size of a harvest cart floated downward, facing the side of the cliff where they'd made camp as the sphere made its descent from above the trees.

The sphere hovered in place before the ivy-covered surface. A clicking noise was heard, and the stone wall parted into two sections with a nearly silent hiss, revealing the alcove situated behind it.

Brilliant, intense light flooded out from the newly exposed enclosure, illuminating the nighttime forest, and casting the sphere's shadow over the hiding place of the searchers. The silvery object then flew up into an open shaft in the ceiling of a room that was now visible, the uncovered doorway within the cliff beginning to slide shut again.

"That could be the resting place of the spirit of the forest. We have to chase that cart, or whatever it is, inside the cliff." Jerod immediately stood and ran toward the two pieces of the wall as they continued to close.

The others hesitated, but then Arthur rose from behind the bushes and ran after Jerod, so Gage and Sean followed. The men gathered in a featureless white room the length and breadth of a half-score of tents, cool air drifting out of the open shaft in the room's ceiling where the flying cart had disappeared. The wall of the cliff closed behind them, blocking egress to the forest.

***

Jerod examined the shaft and then reached into his pack once he had set it down on the cold floor. Jerod removed a fiber rope and slung it over the length of his arms.

"The only way is up through that opening," Jerod observed. "This should be something like scaling the rocky hillsides near Hometown. I didn't think the forest spirit would find rest in the heavens. I thought that underground was more likely."

Jerod swung the rope and caught a strut protruding from the shiny tube at the mouth of the shaft, its hard bone hook attached to the end of the rope. The tube was made of a material the searchers had never seen before but appeared to be something like that of the flying cart.

Jerod tugged at the rope to make sure it was secure. "I'll go first. If I make it to the opening, climb up behind me." Jerod easily scaled the rope, reaching the first strut of the tube that lined the shaft walls, his flowing hair stirred by the circulating air swirling around him.

There were more struts evenly spaced along the side of the tube facing him, and Jerod began to make his way up the shaft to what he hoped would be the top. Gage observed Jerod from the floor and then grasped the dangling rope with his rugged hands, pulling himself to the first strut.

Jerod glanced down and saw that he had made good progress up the tube's shaft. Gage, Arthur, and Sean were gaining on him but appeared small in the distance. Jerod steadied himself, as the scope of the ascent was much greater than he had anticipated. The height he had reached was daunting and could easily cause vertigo in someone less resolute.

The shaft enveloping the tube was as brightly lit as the noonday sun, but Jerod could see no torch or lantern of any kind as he clambered his way up the struts.

Jerod grabbed the last strut before the top of the metallic tube and then hauled himself through its circular opening. He rested for a moment on another cold, smooth floor like the one at the bottom of the shaft, the room as white and featureless as before.

Looking around, Jerod noted that this room was more spacious than the first, with the addition of a single closed door at its far end. In the ceiling of the room, suspended above the metal tube in its own shimmering shaft, was a gray cylinder with many blinking-colored lights, large enough to accommodate several people.

Jerod brought himself to his feet and walked cautiously toward the closed door. The door opened with a whooshing sound as Jerod grew close, disappearing into the wall supporting it.

Jumping back, the unexpected movement startled Jerod. He could see no one on the other side to open the door so suddenly. Jerod breathed deeply of the lush fragrance now washing over him as he took a step forward. What he saw through the open door was an entirely new world, completely outside of his unrefined imagination.

The clatter of Gage reaching the top of the shaft broke Jerod out of his near trance-like state upon seeing the unearthly garden laid out before him. The botanical garden was vast and expansive, marble statuary adorning its avenues and pathways. A cobbled stone path led from the white room's door to a far-off circle at the garden's center.

"Jerod, what do you see?" Gage stood next to Jerod and placed a hand over his brow, the hazy sun from the orange-lit horizon momentarily blinding him. Arthur and Sean joined their fellows at the door, the men deciding to explore the alien setting despite its inherent uncertainty.

The flora and fauna of the garden was unlike any they'd ever seen. Vividly colored insect life fluttered about while enormous, polychromatic birds glided languidly overhead as the searchers strode down the stone path. Everywhere they turned was a new sight, an unfamiliar shade, or an unimagined creature.

"There's the red-and-yellow bird we saw in the forest. Wait. There's three of them by that stone figure." Arthur pointed along the path to a statute of a bare-chested man posing with a shield and spear. The birds rested on the branch of a fruit-bearing tree in full bloom, one bordering the pathway leading toward the center.

Jerod posited, "That bird must've escaped down the tunnel we climbed up. Or maybe the spirit of the forest left it there. This has to be where he makes his home, or else we are in Heaven." Jerod turned to look at his men, but they did not answer him, their eyes wide, attempting to absorb the sensory excess around them.

The searchers came to the central circle, where a synthetic white marble kiosk stood alone, somewhat obscured by light overgrowth from the garden's intrusions over time. Within the empty space of the kiosk's interior was the indentation of a human hand, the impressions of its five fingers splayed evenly around the palm.

"This looks like something the gods would leave for their devoted." Jerod reached out to touch the handprint, but then hesitated, pulling back.

Arthur said, "I'll touch it for you. We might even summon the gods. Wish me luck."

Jerod moved aside, and Arthur reached down to the surface of the kiosk's interior, pressing his own hand firmly into the molding. Flickering blue light filled the vacant space within, and a startled Arthur took a few steps back, bumping into his comrades.

The transparent image of a man dressed in elaborate, tailored clothes took shape over the handprint and began to speak to the searchers, his voice distant and hollow:

"Welcome to the Unearthly Gardens, Deck Eight of the Starship Daedalus. I am the Curator of the botanical gardens, which are modeled after the famed Orto Botanico di Padova. Here, however, we are dedicated to presenting new forms of life which are not indigenous to Old Terra but have been developed exclusively by Strasburger-Ming Industrial Genetics for transport to our eventual destination in the Delta Orionis star system. Please enjoy your visit to these gardens and find peace at this lush oasis in space."

The image of the Curator flickered off and the garden became eerily silent once more, without so much as the sound of a chirping bird. Jerod took on a worried expression and said, "Was that a spirit, or maybe a god? It could have been a vision made from this weird rock. Or maybe it's just magic."

Arthur reassured him, "It's gone now. Some of what the little man said sounded like the words we use, but most of it was only noise. The man did say 'peace,' so this could be a holy place to the gods."

The band wandered among the stagnant fountains and ill-maintained, columnated buildings of the garden, following the stone path to the circular garden's far end. Resting at the path's destination was a glass-paneled building, its exterior frosted from disuse.

"There is a door, but why can we see into the house? Is this magic stone too?" Arthur stepped forward and touched the doorknob of the solitary door leading inside the orchid greenhouse.

The knob was coated with a wet film of some sort that was sticky to his skin and burned slightly. The band entered and was briefly overwhelmed by the thick, humid atmosphere. Orange sunlight filtered weakly through the opaque glass rooftop, dimly lighting the rows of plants spilling out over the walkways.

"This is the farmlands of the gods," Sean said once he had surveyed the open room with its many flowering orchids.

"The gods eat flowers, Sean?" Arthur smirked.

Gage looked down over a row of orchids not far from the doorway after he had walked away from the group.

"That blood flower from the forest is here, too. There is a whole plot of them here."

Jerod stood next to Gage and examined the flower that he had feared touching before. "This is it. The sickly smelling flower that saps the woodlands with its roots. The forest spirit can't be far, my friends."

Arthur called to his fellows from another area of the greenhouse, "I found something too. There is a workplace back here. There are some tools I recognize, but they aren't made of wood or stone. Come and see for yourselves."

At the back of the greenhouse, away from most of the plant life, was a workshop with several synthetic wood tables. The tables, as with the rest of the gardens, were long-neglected and strewn with tools and instruments such as those used in scientific research.

On one of the tables was a plastic tablet with a lid that opened when unlatched. Arthur picked up the tablet and unfastened its lid, placing the lid in the upright position.

As before in the garden, a muted blue light flickered and the holographic image of a man who resembled the Curator appeared on the inner surface as Arthur held it in front of him. The man began to speak, his voice hollow as it had been at the marble kiosk:

"Holo-journal log number 2290-AUG08. I am incrementally adjusting to this new body that was provided by my employers. I agreed

to undergo this procedure to have my conscious mind and my memories imprinted into this artificial facsimile of my youthful self. This construct will allow me to make the lengthy trip to the colonization planet without the need to enter a suspension capsule.

"Most of the crew members and civilian colonists are held in these cryo-capsules, frozen in a state of suspended animation for the duration of the decades-long journey. While the others sleep, I will manage the Unearthly Gardens and continue with my botany studies undisturbed."

The image of the man flickered for a moment, and he then began speaking again, this time dressed in a white lab coat:

"Holo-journal log number 2290-AUG27. Attempted cross-pollination between the two orchid species detailed in holo-journal entry 2289-SEP13. Crosspollination failed to result in a new hybrid species as intended. I will select two new orchid species and reattempt the cross-pollination process, this time isolating for genetic robustness. With more than thirty thousand species and over seventy thousand cultivars, identifying new candidates for cross-pollination should not be an issue."

The image of the man flickered again, but for a few minutes instead of several seconds, as if the tablet was struggling to function correctly. Once the man reappeared and began speaking, his voice sounded panicked, afraid:

"Holo-journal log number 2290-DEC08. There has been a disaster onboard the Daedalus. I have lost contact with the upper decks, and no visitors or human grounds crew have returned since the sudden shock to the vessel.

"The floor of the lab shook violently, with some of my fragile plants being crushed by the falling debris from the greenhouse roof. The grounds of the gardens and my workspace were then bathed in an unnatural light, emitting a dreadful yellow glow for some time after this unex-

pected catastrophe. I am not sure of the nature of the disaster, but I fear the worst."

The image of the man vanished briefly and then returned, his voice stuttering slightly as the avatar flickered in and out:

"Holo-journal log number 2291-MAR11. The long-term health of the garden's flora and fauna is in question after the event. Cellular testing has confirmed that most, if not all, of the lifeforms in the gardens have been altered in some manner after last year's cataclysm. Certain flowering plants have become very aggressive; I have placed these plants on an observation list that is being updated continually.

"I am not sure what the cosmic rays may have done to me as well. My artificial body should be most durable, but that does not seem to be the case. I grow more fatigued with each passing week, more sensitive to sounds and motion outside of my greenhouse. There are plants— carnivorous plants—that I would swear are whispering to me while I tend the gardens. These plants are demanding more food than what I already give them...new kinds of food."

The image of the man flickered and then skipped around, with no intelligible words as he spoke. The tablet stabilized and the man spoke once again, but his appearance was altered from the previous entries. Now, he wore a long cloak, and his hands were not visible:

"Holo-journal log number 2292-OCT21. I have found a solution to the food problem, but it will require the use of the ecology drones stored on Decks Six and Seven. Garden drones presently maintain the Unearthly Gardens and other areas of the ship, but exposure to radiation from the disaster has made their operation unstable. Further cultivation of the Nepenthes rajah hybrid will require securing more drones and more growing space on other decks, some of which seem to be inhabited by survivors."

The holo-journal's final entry recorded no date, and the Curator's face was hidden from view as he spoke, his body covered entirely by the long cloak. His voice had also changed, becoming very thin, even inhuman:

"The drones from the upper decks have been successfully repro-grammed and can now extract mineral wealth from soil in addition to replenishing nutrient depleted soil as was intended with the drones' original programming. The additional nutrients and the other newly acquired food sources will feed it and allow me to join with it to survive on this ship. The only obstacle now is determining a method of shutting down the day and night cycle on the inhabited decks so that it won't be harmed due to the organism's susceptibility to sunlight, even the ship's artificial sunlight."

After the last entry finished, the tablet powered down, its power cell spent. Arthur placed the tablet on the worktable in front of him and saw that his fellows were as badly shaken as he was by the Curator's tale, those parts that could be understood by the searchers.

"Do you smell that?" Arthur then noted the sickeningly sweet odor that they had first inhaled in the forest, which was faintly noticeable in the greenhouse before but was now much stronger. In the gloomy light of the decaying greenhouse, Jerod and his fellows saw a cloaked figure standing silently in the aisle facing them, between the rows of flowering plants.

The figure glided effortlessly towards the band, a rustling sound perceptible along with the overpowering scent of orchids. The figure's cloak opened wide as it approached, and fibrous, tentacled appendages ending in open mouths full of serrated teeth writhed toward the searchers. The last sound Jerod heard was Arthur screaming in terror...

***

Thomas had returned to where the fields met the gentle hills outside of Hometown, the diffuse rays of the late afternoon sun basking over the village. The elders believed that Jerod's band of searchers was lost for good.

Weeks had passed, and they had failed to return from the quest. Elijah attempted to divine their whereabouts, and then suggested sending another expedition, but the council of elders voted it down.

The village's foodstuffs were dwindling faster than anticipated and would not last until the next harvest. Thomas looked up into the mild, sunny sky and noticed something odd. The sun above the village settlement and farmlands seemed to fade very briefly and then refocus, shining once again. Thomas squinted, careful not to look directly into the sun's orb. It happened yet again.

Then, an abrupt darkness. Thomas stumbled about in a panic, the distant cries of the villagers echoing into the void. Thomas inhaled. The sickeningly sweet smell of orchids seeped into the village like a miasma, the only thing discernable in the eternal night of Hometown.

Nao Victoria

Abigail stood at the door to her father's study, her breath coming in short, nervous bursts. She glanced over the ornate carvings in the door's sash, all of which depicted pastoral scenes from the English countryside.

There were images of woods and valleys, shepherds with their flocks, birds in the fields and meadows, and a hunter arching his bow. A ram's head was prominently displayed at the top of the dark mahogany door's solid frame, its curving horns projecting in relief. The rustic scenes were exceptionally detailed, and the door frame was likely older than Abigail's family's home in Wiltshire.

Abigail paused and then rapped on the study door.

"Come in," she heard her father's voice answer in reply.

She cautiously opened the door. Inside, her father was seated at his writing desk, his back to the door. She spoke in her soft child's voice: "Father, Mother said you wanted to see me."

Father turned around to face her, the light of the afternoon sun filtering through the study's partially curtained bay window. "Yes, Abigail, please come in. Come here and stand next to my desk."

Abigail did as she was told. Placed on Father's writing desk among his journals and loose papers was a bell-shaped glass display case resembling the cloches Abigail's mother used in the family garden.

Smiling pleasantly, Father said, "I have something to show you." He lifted the glass dome from its base and took a polished stone, blood-red in color, into the palm of his hand. He held out the stone in front of Abigail, as if offering it to her.

Abigail had always felt apprehension whenever she visited Father's study and personal library, which was not very often. The study was a forbidden place to the rest of the family; Arthur Barrett had always told his daughters to never enter this room without permission. Since the door to the study was nearly always kept locked, Abigail often wondered how he thought she or Evelyn would get in even if they wanted to.

Father closed his fingers tightly around the stone and then squeezed for several moments, all the while wearing a curious expression. When Father relaxed his fingers and displayed the contents of his open palm, a small grey toad rested there. The toad turned in Father's palm and gulped, but made no attempt to leap from its perch onto the study's floor.

Quickly grasping Abigail's right arm, Father deposited the live toad into her palm with his free hand. "Squeeze tightly, Abigail," he murmured. "Don't be afraid; you won't hurt him."

An impassive Abigail did as her Father asked.

"Now, open your hand and look," Father instructed.

Abigail slowly relaxed her fingers from her palm, extending them outward. The polished bloodstone from the display case was in her hand, the toad gone.

Father removed the stone from Abigail's hand and returned it to the display case on his desk. "I have more to teach you," Father said. "You can do so much more than just that, with time."

Abigail looked at her father but said nothing.

"You won't tell your mother or Evelyn about this," Father said sternly. "This is our secret. Once you are older, you will appreciate these gifts."

***

Abigail's mother, Katherine, knelt in her garden, digging into the soil with a trowel. The Barrett family garden occupied a plot just outside of their home in the countryside, which was itself bordered by a low stone wall. Beyond, a cobbled road ran toward the village. The home was some decades old, but many of the family heirlooms and several pieces of furniture had been passed down to Arthur over several generations.

"Mother, what is in the woods across the river? Father said to never venture there." Abigail stood nearby, watching as her mother planted seeds that would grow into vegetables to set the family's dinner table during the coming summer. Abigail held several seedling packets, which she passed to her mother as the woman gestured for them.

"Oh, no one from the village goes there, that's why. A young girl went missing in those woods a while back. And some people before as well. The constable says it's a treacherous place, with sinkholes and the like."

Katherine stood up and brushed dirt from her apron. She looked down at her younger daughter; Abigail was short and slight, with wavy, light blonde hair and large, expressive brown eyes. She bore no close resemblance to either herself, her husband, or to her older sister Evelyn. "Just be a good girl and do as your father says," Katherine said brusquely. "You don't want to get into any trouble once school lets out."

Abigail followed her mother from the garden into the kitchen, observing Katherine as she removed her gardening gloves and washed her hands with a bar of soap in the kitchen sink. There were several weeks left of school before the summer break, and a classmate, Rachel, had asked Abigail to come with her into the woods to do some exploring.

"You're just scared, admit it! Scared of the woods, like a baby," Rachel had said, sticking her tongue out.

"No, I'm not," Abigail retorted anxiously.

"Well, we can't be friends anymore." Rachel made a face and began to walk away after standing from her spot on the park bench next to Abigail. The village's sole schoolyard was not far away.

"Wait, Rachel, please! I'll go. I want to see the woods too, but my father might find out. He told me to stay away."

Rachel stopped in her tracks, turned around slowly, and then smiled. "No, he won't," she said, her eyes flashing mischievously. "We'll leave for the woods right after our classes. We can hide our bicycles in the bushes near the schoolhouse and then slip away once we're dismissed. Our dads will never find out, nor will anyone else."

The thought of entering those woods, even in the daylight, worried Abigail, but Rachel was one of her few friends. Abigail was at the top of their village's small grammar school, and was ostracized by many of the other pupils because of this. She could have even advanced several years to the upper school, but Abigail's parents had decided against it.

Abigail didn't mind; in fact, she preferred to stay where she was. Certain boys at the upper school had long spread rumors concerning Abigail's father. Arthur Barrett was employed as a journalist and writer, with his articles appearing in various newspapers and publications. Word had reached their village that Mr. Barrett had written for "possibly blasphemous" journals printed overseas, with his articles in either French or German instead of English.

Rachel reassured Abigail: "No one wants to go there, so something must be important about the place. We'll just cross the old bridge, take a look around, and then ride back home on our bikes. We'll have hours of light—it's almost summer, after all!"

Abigail said nothing, but gave a sullen nod.

"Let's get back before they miss us," Rachel chirped, as if distracting Abigail from further discussion. She pulled Abigail up from the bench and took off back toward the village school. Classes would resume after lunch, and final exams were coming up in a few weeks' time.

***

"Hide it here, under the arch." Rachel grimaced as she trudged through the mud and leaned her bicycle against the damp stone of the long bridge that connected the village to the secluded woodlands beyond it. Abigail followed, wheeling her bicycle to the hiding place and propping it near Rachel's. This done, she turned to Rachel, as if awaiting instruction.

Rachel took a sack from her bike's iron basket and opened it to show Abigail the wax paper-wrapped sandwiches inside. "I nabbed these from the school canteen right before we left," she said, handing a sandwich to Abigail. "I'm faster than I look, eh?"

Abigail unwrapped a sandwich and took a bite.

Rachel had already gobbled hers down and was speeding up the river's embankment toward the bridge above. The old stone bridge was not well maintained, but it was solidly built. It had been here for as long as Abigail could remember, and for many years before that.

Unbeknownst to the girls or indeed to any of the villagers, the forest had once been home to a small settlement of shepherds and goat herders. The community had since been abandoned for reasons unknown.

Having caught up with her friend, Abigail peered across to the head of the bridge. It was a warm, cloudy day, the first of summer. Abigail wouldn't be noticed missing until hours from now when Mother would call her for the family dinner.

The forest appeared vast, almost endless, a thick canopy of deciduous trees and rolling hills stretching as far as they could see. Near the end of the bridge was a narrow, partially submerged path leading away into the forest.

"This way," Rachel said, following the path.

Abigail hurried behind her.

The two girls wandered for some time, the bramble undergrowth soon giving way to scores of broad oak trees, their low branches tangled together. The oaks' exposed roots intertwined over the barely visible pathway, slowing the girls' progress. Rachel climbed the raised roots in front of her as she advanced, appearing determined to penetrate to the heart of the woods itself.

After a long while, Abigail stopped. "This is just a deserted place, Rachel. Nothing is here." She wavered briefly and then said, "My mother told me a girl from the village was never found after coming into these woods by herself."

Rachel paused on the path before turning. "She was my cousin, Mary." She showed no emotion as she spoke.

Abigail looked at Rachel in surprise, waiting for her to continue.

"You wouldn't know her—she went to the upper school. It happened when we were quite young. I just wanted to see where it all took place. She'll never be found now."

Abigail's face fell, and she stepped forward to lay a hand on her friend's shoulder. "Rachel, I'm sorry. I only thought you wanted to come here as a dare, for some excitement. I didn't know this was personal for you."

Rachel sat down on the moss-covered roots of a towering oak, a tree that had perhaps seen the previous millennium as a sapling. She looked about the depths of the woods, surveying the maze of trees that stretched in all directions around her.

"You're right," she said after a long moment, her voice strangely quiet, "we should go back. I'm not sure what I wanted to find here, but now I've seen it."

Forcing a smile, Rachel stood and began tracing the path in front of her. Abigail watched her for a moment and made as if to follow, when something caught her eye in the hollow beneath the sprawling oak where Rachel had been seated.

The cavity at the base of the oak contained something. Abigail squinted in the shade, but the hollow was deep and dark, defying the late afternoon sunlight. She approached, crouching beside the roots, and then reached into the oak's dank cavity. It was no good—her arm wasn't long enough. Sighing, Abigail sat back against the oak's roots.

"Rachel, there's something here."

When no response came, Abigail rose, glancing around. She peered down the path Rachel had taken. Nothing.

Pleading under her breath, Abigail took off after her friend. She followed the obscured path for what felt like hours, finally stumbling into a natural formation almost entirely concealed by hanging moss and overgrowth. The formation had an entrance like that of a small cave.

Why didn't we see this the first time through? Abigail thought to herself. *Rachel might be playing a trick on me. Oh, I hope not. There might not even be a Cousin Mary.*

She stepped off the path among the trees and came to the formation's entrance, staring into its dim passageway. The distant sounds of dripping water echoed from somewhere deep inside, and the air within felt cool after the warm summer breeze of the woods. Abigail decided this was a place from which someone might pull a joke on her, so she went in.

The smooth stone passage ended in a woodland grotto, open to the sky above, overgrown, but clearly once used for some purpose. At the center of the grotto was a strange statue. No one else was there.

I hope Rachel didn't fall into one of those crevices Mother warned me about, Abigail thought.

The stone sculpture was very detailed. The figure stood on a pedestal, which was clearly delved from the same quarry as the statue itself. A representation of a bearded, hair-covered man with spiral horns and hooved goat legs, the figure held a set of pipes. Recalling Father's books, Abigail recognized the statue as a Roman faun from classical antiquity.

Has this statue been here since that time? Abigail wondered. *A work of art should be in a museum in London, not out in the woods where no one can see it.*

As she studied the faun's finely wrought face, something moved in the corner of her eye. The wind awoke, the branches of the sturdy elms and green shrubs of the grotto swaying, the clouds above swelling overcast and perilous as they traveled swiftly overhead. The statue extended its arms and placed the set of pipes to its lips. As Abigail staggered back, it began to play a haunting melody.

The song of the pipes drowned out the ominous rumbling of the gathering storm above, its music fixing Abigail in place. Thunder cracked and the winds whipped around her as the eerie yet seductive song swelled to a crescendo. Abigail tore her eyes away, spying something at the grotto's end—an unmoving Rachel spread out on a stone stab, lightning bursting in the sky above her.

Held fast by the pipes' song, Abigail walked to the altar of sacrifice and took in hand the ceremonial blade which rested at the base of the slab. Her wide, staring eyes looked down at the motionless form of Rachel—she was laid on her back, exposed and vulnerable. Tears swelling in her eyes, Abigail felt herself raise the ancient dagger over her head . . .

Evelyn opened her eyes sleepily and looked across at her sister's bed, upon which someone was resting. The curtained window was open, the moonlight shining in from the otherwise lightless country night. Abigail was facing her sister, a blanket draped over her, fast asleep.

Springing from her bed, Evelyn pulled the blanket from Abigail, tossing it to the bedroom floor. Her sister stirred, rolling over from her pillow to look up at Evelyn, still half-asleep.

"Where have you been?" Evelyn hissed angrily. "Mother and Father drove to the village and told the constable you never came home after school. There are men out looking for you at this moment."

Abigail sat up and rubbed her eyes without saying anything, her legs dangling over the side of the bed. In the dim light of the bedroom, Evelyn could see Abigail was still wearing her school dress, which was badly torn and soiled.

"Where am I?" Abigail finally said, her voice barely a whisper.

"You're at home, in our bedroom," replied Evelyn, frowning. "What in God's name happened to you?"

Abigail looked up at Evelyn for the first time and said, "I don't know." Evelyn turned on the nightstand lamp and saw Abigail's shoes lying at the foot of the bed, covered in mud. There was a trail of dirt from the bedroom window to where Abigail had slept.

The sisters heard a door creak open in the house and then hurried footsteps toward the hallway outside of their room. The bedroom door was flung open without warning.

"Abigail!" Katherine exclaimed, running toward the bed and hugging her daughter tightly. "I'm so glad you're safe! We'll let Constable Jarvis know that we've found you." She pushed Abigail away and held her at arm's distance, inspecting her daughter's face and clothes. "But the constable said your friend Rachel is missing as well. Where is she?"

Abigail gazed sluggishly at her mother and then her sister, as if confused by the question. "I can't remember," she said in a dead tone. "I don't even remember how I came home."

Father was now standing in the doorway dressed in his pajamas and slippers, his robe tied at the waist.

"Enough of this. Abigail, go back to sleep once your mother dresses you in your bedclothes." Father shut the bedroom window abruptly, making sure the window latch was locked in place. "I will call on the constable first thing in the morning. The search party can't be reached tonight—not unless I go looking for them myself." With that, he turned and marched from the room.

Katherine began to remove Abigail's dress, and Evelyn took some of her sister's nightclothes out of a drawer. Katherine paused as she lifted the torn dress Abigail was wearing over her daughter's head. She didn't say anything but pulled Abigail's bare arm toward the nightstand's lamp.

There were faint claw marks along her daughter's forearm, as if left by some large animal.

***

"Constable Jarvis discovered your bicycle next to Rachel's under a bridge today. The same bridge to the woods your father and I warned you not to enter." Katherine was somber as she relayed the news to Abigail. "This means you could be implicated in a crime if Rachel isn't found, even as a young girl."

Abigail positioned herself on a stool in the kitchen, listening to her mother intently. Abigail looked out the kitchen window and saw Evelyn working in the family garden. *Where is Father?* she thought.

She met her mother's eyes. "How, Mother? Rachel and I are friends—I loved her dearly."

"The constable's men will continue to search for Rachel, but it was explained to me there is the possibility of a criminal case if any more evidence against you is found. I will pray for both of us."

Katherine studied Abigail. She knew her young daughter couldn't have anything to do with Rachel's disappearance. Yes, her selective amnesia was disconcerting, but her condition, real or feigned, didn't mean she had actually harmed her friend.

"You can't recall how your bike ended up under the bridge? You were riding home from school, you stopped by the side of the road with Rachel, and then the next thing you remember is waking up in your bedroom at night?"

"Yes, Mother, that's all I remember. Now may I please go outside with Evelyn?" Abigail dropped from the stool and stood near the kitchen table, waiting to be dismissed.

"Go. But dinner will be ready in a few hours—once your father returns. The constable will want to speak with you again in a couple of days when the search is concluded." Katherine watched her daughter open the kitchen's side door and join her sister in the garden. There were already insinuations being made in the village about this apparent tragedy, with some of the villagers singling out Abigail as the culprit.

"You're a witch!" One of the boys threw a stone at Abigail, but it missed her, striking the tree behind instead. "And you killed Rachel!" Several older boys with handfuls of stones had cornered Abigail outside the schoolyard against a shady tree. Abigail moved to walk past them, but they blocked her exit.

"I'm telling Mrs. Thorpe!" Abigail cried out. She became very frightened as the three boys glared down at her and, despite herself, she began to cry. One of the boys turned and swore under his breath. Mrs. Thorpe was walking toward them at a brisk pace, her face as fearsome as ever. "It's that old bag, Mrs. Thorpe. Just walk away, don't look at her," he commanded.

Quickly, the boys slipped behind the tree where Abigail was cornered and then away from the school grounds.

"Abigail, are you all right?" Mrs. Thorpe crouched down beside her. "Do you know those boys' names? What class are they in?"

"No, but . . ." Abigail hesitated. This wasn't the first such incident. Most of the children at school had coolly ignored Abigail after Rachel disappeared, their parents telling them Abigail may have been to blame after word circulated through the village. Now, with yet another reason to resent her, their coldness was apparently turning to outright hostility. The last thing Abigail wanted was more trouble.

"No," she corrected herself, "I don't know who they are. They're in another class, but I'm not sure which one. I didn't get a good look at them as it happened so fast."

Mrs. Thorpe frowned, but decided not to push the matter. She moved to calm Abigail and said, "Just come back to the yard. You need to collect your things before heading home. You must let me know if something like this happens again."

Abigail watched as Mrs. Thorpe walked back to gather the other children in the schoolyard and lead them back inside. She reached down and picked up the stone that had nearly struck her from the foot of the tree. Red-faced from crying, Abigail squeezed tightly, then released her hand. The small grey toad croaked, and Abigail placed it into her dress pocket before walking back to the village school.

***

Abigail pressed her ear against her parent's bedroom door. The hallway was dark—she was supposed to be asleep. Mother and Father had been arguing, so she'd crept down the hall to find out if they were discussing anything that might involve her. Evelyn was still deep in slumber, oblivious to her parents' raised voices.

"I've never felt right about Abigail. You know that, Arthur. Even my pregnancy with her was quite . . . difficult."

There was a pause.

"There were terrible nightmares up until her birth. You must remember how it was. I vowed I would never have another child after Abigail."

"Yes, but the doctor said nothing was wrong with you, at least not physically," Arthur replied. "He said it was all depression from a second pregnancy so soon after your first."

Abigail peered through the keyhole and caught a glimpse of her father trying to pull her mother close, only for her to move to the other side of their bed, glancing away from him.

"But here is the good news I promised you," her father continued, undeterred, "I've accepted an editorial position with *The Daily Sentinel*, the paper I told you about when we first considered moving away from Wiltshire. Relocating overseas will require applying for family passports, visas, and eventually new citizenship once we're settled in."

Katherine turned to face him again, and he smiled at her hopefully. "Arthur, I couldn't be more happy," she said, smiling weakly. "We need a fresh start after all of this. Even our friends no longer see us. We're not welcome here anymore."

She embraced her husband, and they sat down on the bed, Katherine resting her head on Arthur's shoulder.

"This is a permanent move; we'll be far away from Wiltshire," Arthur said, caressing Katherine's hair. "A new life in a new country. I'll be in the study for a while to go over some of the details. Try to get some sleep; I'll join you soon."

Abigail backed away as if struck and quickly dodged down the hallway, silently slipping into her bedroom and leaping into bed. A moment later, Arthur's head appeared in the bedroom doorway. He glanced at each bed in turn and, apparently satisfied, continued on toward his study.

He sat at his writing desk and reviewed the family's travel documents, considering how taking Abigail away from Wiltshire had changed the plans he had for her. Abigail would still one day reach her full potential under his tutelage as an Ovate. Too many of the villagers and local authorities had begun to suspect the truth—or at least part of it, including Katherine.

Arthur stood and selected a black leather-bound volume from among the many books lining the shelves of his study. The weighty tome was centuries old, with a golden sickle on its spine.

Returning to his desk, Arthur began to quietly read aloud, murmuring in a strange language. The wind outside the study's bay window stirred, the sudden rush of night air rattling the aged glass of its windowpanes.

Katherine lay on her bed half-asleep, breathing lightly. She reflected on the move from Wiltshire. Life in a new country, her husband with a new position, and a fresh start away from the enmity and social isolation that had plagued their family these last months.

Abigail must have gone into those woods, she thought, but could she really be the cause of Rachel's disappearance? Shortly before she realized she was pregnant with Abigail, and then throughout the term of her pregnancy, Katherine had suffered from a recurrent nightmare: a grove in the woods at twilight, a stone slab, and shadowy forms surrounding her.

Each time, the nightmare would play out in the same manner. Barefoot and in a sheer white gown, she would lie on the stone slab. A man (or was it a man?) appeared from among the dark forms and stood before her. She would awaken just as the man had knelt over her, reaching out with a clawed hand . . .

The first time the nightmare came upon her, she'd awoken the next morning with odd scratches on her arms and legs, but the marks had quickly faded. Afterward, she'd begun to feel a visceral craving for raw meat and organs from the butcher's, the purchases of which she hid from Arthur. Sharp pains, as if she were being kicked by some hooved animal inside her, persisted through the pregnancy, even though the doctor could find nothing wrong.

Katherine lay on her back, touching her stomach as she recalled her fear the unborn child would suffer a deformity or even be monstrous once delivered. But Abigail had been perfectly healthy as a baby—beautiful, even.

Yet there was always the lingering suspicion that something was wrong with Abigail. The moments when Katherine would catch her daughter studying her while they worked together in the garden or in the kitchen, a puzzling expression on her face. Abigail's frequent nighttime walks alone these last few years, and the sometimes-fitful sleeps she endured, waking Katherine in the middle of the night to find her daughter wide-eyed and terrified. Could Abigail, this lovely young girl, truly be a murderess?

Abigail was asleep, tucked up warmly in her bed. Outside her bedroom window, amid the moaning winds, the cloaked figure of a tall man stood in silence. The outline of stag's antlers protruded sharply from the tall man's head as he stared in through the window at Abigail. Abigail continued to sleep, oblivious to the man's presence.

***

Abigail peered around at Father's new study, which had been left open and unlocked. She held an oakwood cane across her lap, the length of which she examined, running her hand over its burnished shaft. The cane wore a silver metal handle in the shape of a ram's head with horns. She could hear her mother, who'd just been on the telephone, sobbing in the nearby living room.

The crying stopped. A moment later, Katherine walked into the study. Abigail quickly hid her father's cane under the writing desk.

"We will likely have to move to a rented home soon, Abigail," Katherine said, her eyes almost bloodshot. "I won't be able to keep up with the mortgage now that your father is gone. I'm sorry. I wanted better for you and your sister."

She let herself fall in front of Abigail's chair and hugged her child close, tears leaking down her cheeks. Finally, she straightened, sniffed, and dabbed at her eyes. "It's getting late. Go upstairs and get some rest. Evelyn is already asleep. The doctor gave me enough sedatives for her to last the next month."

Abigail slipped from the plush chair and stood in front of her mother, giving her a faint smile, as if to assent. Her mother slipped past her, and Abigail heard the bathroom door down the hallway shut, followed by sounds of incessant crying.

Out the study's window, the spacious yard stretched behind the house, obscured from their neighbors by rows of oak trees on either side. Mother had found Father hanging from a branch by a knotted rope among the copse of oaks at the yard's far end. The police had removed Father's body from the tree before Abigail and Evelyn had arrived home from school.

The night before, Father had called Abigail to his study in the family's new home, coming first to her room where she'd been reading alone. Father had seemed very distraught, his eyes wide with fear, his face pallid and grieved.

She'd followed him to his study, noting the heavy curtains of its picture window were drawn, blocking the panoramic view of the back garden. A jumbled pile of books lay on Father's desk, a black book with a gold sickle on its spine being the most prominent. It was as if the books had been torn from the study's shelves in a panic and then searched through, one after the other.

Arthur took Abigail by both arms. "Abigail, I'm not sure how to tell you this, but I must. You have a very special gift. Not one received from me, but from your real father." His breath came in ragged gasps, but he composed himself enough to continue: "There are sacraments of evil as well as of good in all of us, but how we choose to use these graces determines our fates. There are also places where shadows and the dwellers of twilight reach out to touch this world, if only imperceptibly. I started you on a path that may lead to a world of shadows, but—for your own sake—choose a different one once I am gone."

Holding a trembling hand to Abigail's cheek, Arthur kissed her goodnight. Finally, he led her to the study's door and then locked himself inside. Abigail returned to her bedroom to sleep.

Now, she rose from the writing desk and unlatched the study's back door. She walked to the sheltered copse where Arthur had hanged himself by the neck. There, among the oak trees, stood the Horned God. He embraced Abigail, and she embraced him in return.

About the Author

James Dermond is a writer who lives in Colorado. Intrigued from a very young age by horror anthologies and the short story form, this book is his latest modest contribution to the genre.

Doorways to the Unseen 10: 6 Tales of Terror and Suspense is the tenth volume in a series of short story collections. The eleventh volume in the series will be published in October 2025.

To sign up for free eBooks and other future giveaways, please subscribe to James Dermond's author website here:

www.jamesdermond.com

James Dermond's Amazon Author Page
https://www.amazon.com/James-Dermond/e/B01M1S54YP

James Dermond's Goodreads Author Page
https://www.goodreads.com/author/show/15862747.James_Dermond

James Dermond on Facebook
https://www.facebook.com/JamesDermondAuthor/

James Dermond on Twitter

JAMES DERMOND

https://twitter.com/JamesDermond

Prologue

T hank you for reading this latest volume in the short horror story series, Doorways to the Unseen! We are now on volume ten of what will eventually become a twelve-volume series of books. The planned publication schedule is two volumes every year, with the final volume released in April 2026. A multi-volume hardcover edition of the collected stories would then be released in October of the same year.

If you enjoyed this collection of stories, please leave a review on Amazon and other online bookstores where volumes in the Doorways to the Unseen series can be found. A positive review will help promote the book and inform other readers of the book's merits.

www.ingramcontent.com/pod-product-compliance
Lightning Source LLC
Chambersburg PA
CBHW020421130626
46549CB00006B/2678